Before The Earth That Was

BRICE BARRERE

TRAFFORD

Canada • UK • Ireland • USA • Spain

© Copyright 2004, Brice Barrere.
All rights reserved.

No part of this publication may be reproduced, stored in a retrieval system, or transmitted, in any form or by any means, electronic, mechanical, photocopying, recording, or otherwise, without the written prior permission of the author.

Note for Librarians: a cataloguing record for this book that includes Dewey Decimal Classification and US Library of Congress numbers is available from the National Library of Canada. The complete cataloguing record can be obtained from the National Library's online database at:
www.nlc-bnc.ca/amicus/index-e.html
ISBN 1-4120-2750-0
Printed in Victoria, BC, Canada

TRAFFORD

Offices in Canada, USA, Ireland, UK and Spain
This book was published *on-demand* in cooperation with Trafford Publishing. On-demand publishing is a unique process and service of making a book available for retail sale to the public taking advantage of on-demand manufacturing and Internet marketing. On-demand publishing includes promotions, retail sales, manufacturing, order fulfilment, accounting and collecting royalties on behalf of the author.
Books sales in Europe:
Trafford Publishing (UK) Ltd., Enterprise House, Wistaston Road Business Centre, Wistaston Road, Crewe CW2 7RP
UNITED KINGDOM
phone 01270 251 396 (local rate 0845 230 9601)
facsimile 01270 254 983; info.uk@trafford.com
Book sales for North America and international:
Trafford Publishing, 6E–2333 Government St.,
Victoria, BC V8T 4P4 CANADA
phone 250 383 6864 (toll-free 1 888 232 4444)
fax 250 383 6804; email to bookstore@trafford.com

www.trafford.com/robots/04-0578.html

10 9 8 7 6 5 4 3 2

PREFACE

BEFORE THE EARTH THAT WAS

Our purpose for this work is multiple. First, we would like to write Christian literature that is both informative and enjoyable reading. Secondly, we wish to introduce the layman to the Gap Theory. Even though it is a very old theory, few have even heard of it.

We also wish to set forth the truth of creation over evolution. We will not; however, ignore such things as subhuman fossils, which have to be taken into consideration. True, some are fake; however, some are not and have to be accounted for.

Also, angels have been placed on such a high plane that some even worship them. We hope to show them more as they are in reality. Job 4:18 (NKJV) says God charges His angels with error. We see that they are not perfect creatures! In Psalms 82:7 (NKJV), God, speaking to fallen angels, says they shall die like men. So angels can even die! The belief is common that since God made them "spirits," that they, and even God, Himself, don't have bodies. In fact, their bodies are made out of spiritual flesh. Their bodies would be similar to the one that Jesus had after His resurrection, and before

He took on human flesh. In angelic warfare, they could even kill each other!

Lucifer was the most perfect angel ever created, but he was stupid enough to sin and think he could get away with it. He was also imperfect enough to place self before common sense. Thus, we see that they aren't something to be placed on a plane up close to God. Respect them, yes. Worship them—NO! In our fallen state, they are much higher and more glorious than we are. We were, however, created to attain a higher plane than they are on.

We also hope to explain Lucifer to have been a past high priest as shown in Ezekiel 28.

We would like to go into the Gap Theory a little more right here.

Genesis 1:1 portrays God creating the universe out of nothing! The Hebrew word bara, used in this verse, means to call into being without the aid of pre-existing material.

In the Hebrew, verse one is set apart from verse two. Verse two is connected to verse one in the King James Version of the Bible by "and." "And" is not in the original.

In the creation of the first six days, the word "asah" is used, and it means to build out of existing material.

Without form in verse two comes from the word "tohu" and should be rendered ruin-desolation. Void comes from "bohu" and means emptiness. We have an empty desolation—a ruin. Many translations include the word 'waste'.

Isaiah 45:18 says God did not create Earth a tohu! The same word is used in Jeremiah 4:23, where it is said that Jerusalem would be without form and void, a tohu! A ruin and desolation; not created that way, caused to be that way!

Job pictures the Pre-Adamic deluge in Job 9:4-7. Verse

eight shows the Spirit moving upon the waters prior to the six days creation.

Psalms 82 depicts God giving the fallen angels one last chance to shape up.

In Ezekiel 28:12-19 we see quickly that we aren't speaking to any mortal. This creature is too perfect to be human. If that isn't enough, he has been in Eden. He is a king, a ruler. He wears jewels. Where else do we find jewels worn like this? The Hebrew priests wore them! This fellow is a priest! He is also a cherub that sinned, and a high-ranking one at that. He had access to the throne. God is going to destroy him, and his sin was selfishness. No, we didn't misspeak. Yes, He fell from pride, however, pride is just one facet of selfishness. EVERY sin can be traced back to selfishness! He was not only a priest, but he defiled his temple. He apparently didn't usurp the throne, for he had a choice between right and wrong. This can be none other than the devil, himself! When was Satan ever a priest and a king? He hasn't been since Genesis 1:1. It had to be pre-adamic!

Before The Earth That Was

Part One

CHAPTER I

THE THRONE ROOM

Light! Beautiful light! Multicolored light! One thought of every color and shade of oil paint swirling in crystal clear water. Yes, it was clear, beautiful, and easy on the eye. Gold and silver flecks danced in this wonderful air. The air appeared to be of two different types, and as oil and water won't mix, neither would these. As the air flowed, the colors of each type seemed to mix and then change when they came into contact with their own kind. They were always forming new patterns and colors as they would have if oil paint floated upon water. Yet it was an illusion. It was air, not oil and water! No, it didn't cause any eye strain, in fact, the eye found it quite restful.

Two mighty angels stepped through the veil, which appeared to be soft, flexible, spun gold. They stopped, overwhelmed by the sheer beauty in spite of their familiarity with the scene. Two warrior cherubim, splendid in their own excellence, stood with their wings touching over the throne itself. The throne was a huge sapphire[1]. It was cut in such a way that seated in the center was God the Father. He was flanked on the left by God the Holy Spirit, and on the right by God the Son (Jehovah in the Old Testament—Jesus in the New Testament). Yes, and Jehovah—The Son, possessed a very real body of Spiritual flesh. The three made one just as we are a three-part being but are still one. Blended, they become the one triune God just as our body, soul, and spirit makes up the individual.

The fantastic sapphire stood upon a flat diamond. The beautiful diamond was cut in such a manner as to form the floor of the throne room. Its composition seemed to be living flame. It was consolidated flame, yet it flowed beneath one's feet in the midst of the thick, transparent stone floor. The light from the flame was reflected up from the brazen altar beneath. At the foot of the throne, the floor was carpeted with what looked like the same spun gold that the veil was made of. It was softer than any fabric on Earth.

Tapestries which seemed to be made of woven light hung on the walls. They changed patterns and scenes even as one watched them. Exotic, beautiful grained woods gave off odors which pleased the sense of smell without being overpowering. Added to the wood smells was incense of the same type as would later burn in the earthly tabernacle. It sent up wafts of smoke from exotic censors. Gold sparkled everywhere, either as the entire objects or as caps and overlay for such things as ivory, furniture, certain wooden objects, even some metal fixtures. Seven golden shafts about two inches in diameter formed a half circle out about thirty feet from the foot of the throne. These shafts were topped by what looked like golden buds of flowers. The buds looked to be about half opened and from them tongues of cloven flame danced and flickered. This was the abode of the omnipresent sevenfold Holy Spirit, Who also sat on the throne to complete that unit.

Standing just within the veil, were two exquisite, and beautiful cherubim. At first glance, the only difference between them and any other cherubim were the light, but beautiful crowns they wore. In their right hands were magnificent scepters, which were as long as the cherubim were tall. They were made out of ivory, which was capped and decorated with gold and precious jewels.

If we had been watching them, we would have been shocked when one turned its head to look to the side. When facing Michael and Gabriel, all they saw were their handsome human faces; however, the back of their heads contained the face of a lion!

Just as the human faces of the four creatures were symbolical of the humanity of Jesus, and their lion faces were symbolical of the kingship of Jesus, these creatures symbolized Him as the king who would reign on Earth during the Millennium. Their spirits were in such fine tune to the Spirit of God that they knew who to extend their scepters to. Of course, they were always extended to Michael and Gabriel.

Jehovah spoke lovingly to the two messengers. "Come, Gabriel and Michael, We have electrifying news for you to spread throughout the realm of Heaven. As you know, the creation of the angelic host is all but complete. There is still, however, one more angel to create. He will be the Covering Cherub[2], the Supreme Commander of all angels of all ranks. He will be in charge of music, and will be the very bodyguard of God. He will also be the mediator for the creation we plan for the future on Earth. In short, he will be the greatest, the ultimate of our angelic creation. His name shall be Lucifer!

"Now, get moving, fellows. We won't create him until all have gathered. This will be a gala celebration, and We want none to miss it."

Gabriel and Michael fell upon their faces in heart felt adoration. Gabriel exclaimed, "Oh thank you, Holy Father. The leadership of this angel is so needed!"

Rising to leave, Michael all but fell over Creature[3], Who, along with Beastie, had overheard and were also giving vocal thanks. Gabriel reached over and patted Beastie's four faced head. His human face smiled, the lion face purred like a contented pussy cat, the ox face lowed, and the eagle blinked knowingly. Gabriel and Michael walked out chuckling as they went.

Michael's handsome features displayed the wonder he felt. "Gabe, I wouldn't have believed that you could improve on the atmosphere of the throne room."

"Yes, Mike, that anything could be done to enhance the Mountain of God would have seemed remote. But with the addition of Lucifer, we should reach new heights of love, joy, and holiness."

"You bet! And don't forget beauty in all its phases! The music alone should just be beyond comprehension!"

Gabriel's tone became businesslike. "OK, pal, let's split up. We can send everyone we meet to spread the word. Sort of a chain reaction, you might say. It won't take long to blanket the realm."

The faces of the first bunch Gabriel approached lit up, but the second didn't seem to be enthusiastic about spreading the news. A small, rather plump angel with a pointed, receding chin, and squeaky voice, whined, "How come God doesn't just speak the word so all will hear? Why do we have to run all over Heaven?"

"Beelzebub,[4]"replied Gabriel, "you know we are used because God chooses to do His will through His creatures. Why our very name, angel, means messenger. If He had wanted to use His power in the way you suggest, we wouldn't even have been necessary. You should be thankful He does use us!"

"Yes, I suppose so," sighed Beelzebub, without conviction, "but, it does seem such a waste of time and energy. Now let me get this straight. God is going to create another 'Great Angel'; one that is better than He's ever come up with?" asked Beelzebub.

A certain amount of righteous indignation crossed Gabriel's face. "Beelzebub, you are starting to stretch my patience. Beware that you don't stretch God's."

Beelzebub's face screwed up like a pouting child's and he whined, "Oh, I wouldn't do that. I only asked a question."

Gabriel's expression had become angry as he snapped, "Look fella, this is not just another 'Great angel! This is the 'Greatest Angel', and he's to be perfect in every way. Now, get the message out!"

He spun on his heal to end the conversation. As he was leaving, it seemed he heard someone in the group mutter, "Just what we always needed, another Great Angel."

Michael had been hurrying from group to group and angel to angel energetically, when he ran into a tall, Broad shouldered, muscular angel called Apollyon[5]. Michael spoke to him pleasantly, but Apollyon never even looked up. Michael spoke again, and the big angel growled, "Yah, I heard you the first time. Can't you see I'm busy?"

Michael controlled his annoyance and replied, "Look, friend, these are orders from Jehovah, and they're quite important."

"All right, Mickey, have your say and get out of here."

It was a testimony to Michael's righteous character that he proceeded to give his message quickly and briefly, and left in respect for Apollyon's wishes. As a matter of fact, Apollyon wasn't any more pleased than Michael was for him to move on.

At last, the message had traveled throughout the realm, and angels were gathering in clusters in the District of Eden[6]. Some of the higher-ranking ones were actually in the Garden of God.

Gabriel and Michael had both returned. They were in the Garden of God, seated under the Tree of Life. They were staring absently into the River of Life as it flowed past their feet. The largest part of the holy beings around them were in a festive mood, but there was a smaller crowd that didn't seem so happy.

The moods of Gabriel and Michael were unusual. They too, were rather sober, and in deep conversation.

Musingly, Michael said, "Gabe, I don't quite understand the attitude of some of our brothers."

Gabriel was silent for a few moments, then reflected, "True, Mike, I don't either; and I can't say that I like what I see."

Michael looked up earnestly, "I'll tell you what I haven't seen, and I thank God for it. I haven't seen anyone in the realm who is capable of consolidating guys like Beelzebub and Apollyon. Give them a leader, and I can't even comprehend the problems that would arise."

Michael's gaze encompassed the crowd, and he continued, "Well, it appears that all have arrived. Now you as 'He who stands in the presence of God', and I as 'The Commander-in-Chief of the Armies of Heaven', are about due to report in the Holy of Holies. Do you suppose we should relate our fears to the Heavenly Father?"

"It just might be a good idea, at least, it will put our minds at ease."

Turning toward the entrance to the Holy Place, through which one had to pass before entering the throne room, their eyes naturally picked up the trail which wound from where they were seated to the ornate gate. The trail gleamed brightly and for good reason. Shimmering coals gave off flames which ranged from yellow to blue and green. The trail was fringed with what looked like stones, but really were pieces of super heated brass.

As they stepped onto the fiery path, Gabriel spoke musingly, "Isn't it interesting that there are none of us who are pure enough to enter the Holy of Holies without being purified by fire."

Michael nodded and added, "Yes, and that there are actually so few of us who are pure enough to be cleansed enough by any means to approach the Father."

Again, the two friends paused as they entered. As always, they were struck afresh by the unimaginable grandeur of the place. With bowed heads they fell at the feet of their God in adoration.

Leaning forward with a smile, Jehovah ordered, "Up boys, you don't speak to plainly with your mouths in the carpet. Let's hear your report."

As they arose and thought of their experiences, both looked a little troubled.

Jehovah, seeing their countenances, spoke again, "What troubles you, My sons? Have all gathered?"

"Yes, my Lord," said Gabriel, "they have gathered; however, the attitude of some seems both disrespectful and almost hostile. We thought it best to bring this to Your attention. We realize that You know all things, but this way you can put our minds at ease."

"Ah," God murmured, "yes, the time draws near."

Michael looked even more troubled, "You mean this is all part of Your plan?" he asked[7].

A look of sadness crossed the Lord's face as He returned, "Look, Michael, if you elect to run somewhere, knowing that at some point, you will stub your toe, but you still wish to run, and do so; you have included stubbing your toe in your plan. I am ordering certain events and allowing certain others which result as a consequence of My action. Relax, My friends, I am in complete control; and it is best if you don't know any more at present

"Now make ready for the creation of Lucifer. It will be done in the outer court where all can see. Gabriel, sound your horn to bring the assembly together!"

CHAPTER II

LUCIFER

The blast pealed forth from Gabriel's trumpet, and an expectant hush fell over the spacious outer court.

The dazzling Shekinah cloud rose from the Holy of Holies, and all knew that The Father was leaving the throne. Coming out into the Holy Place, He burst upon the waiting angels in all His brilliant glory.

Without exception, all fell to their knees. Whether from love or fearful respect, none could stand in the presence of Almighty God.

With love virtually emanating from His being, He commanded, "Rise and make yourselves comfortable, My Children."

The silence was tangible as all stood with bated breath. With ringing shout of command, Jehovah cried, "Lucifer, stand forth!"

A roaring cheer arose and then the angels broke into song. Myriads of voices joined in music of such beauty and quality that the hair on Michael's neck stood on end.

Stepping out of the Shekinah glory was the most beautiful angel in creation.

The host of the Lord surged forward, grasping Lucifer's hand, hugging him, and displaying their love, affection and loyalty. Already, he was their leader.

One look at his face showed that the display had touched him to the center of his spirit. His face fairly beamed.

Jehovah noticed, as did Michael and Gabriel, that the beautiful Archangel did not even offer to give the Lord the glory.

The two angels gave him the benefit of the doubt. After all, he had just been created. No doubt after he had stood in the Holy of Holies, hearing the wisdom of God as he would, he would reach perfection.

For a period of time, the whole of Heaven was one gala festival. At last, however, the party was over, and the entire Godhead was back in the Holy of Holies. Practically all Heaven was clustered about Lucifer. Oh yes, there were exceptions. Two old friends were lounging in the presence of the Father on the Mountain of God, absorbing love, knowledge, and understanding.

Some time after Lucifer's creation, God beckoned to Michael and Gabriel who were visiting with one of the double-faced cherubim. "Come here, fellas, I've got another job for you. I've given Lucifer time to come of his own accord, but it seems he isn't going to do so. Would you boys go tell him that We wish to begin his training and would like his presence on the Mountain of God immediately?"

The two Archangels were more than ready to go as neither had really gotten a chance to become acquainted with the new angel leader. Both looked forward to fellowshiping with him while he learned the fine points of leadership from the author of leadership, Jehovah God. They were sure that what had been a wonderful friendship between two mighty archangels would now include the mightiest one of all.

It did not take long to find him. All they had to do was gravitate to the largest crowd of angels they could see. There he was in the midst, mesmerizing them with his supernatural oratory. They, too, listened in awe, feeling unworthy to break in on him.

Finally, Michael, the typical soldier, put orders ahead of feelings. He stepped up, and spoke respectfully to the mighty angel.

"Sir—"

For a moment, annoyance crossed Lucifer's dark handsome face. His built in diplomacy came to his rescue instantly, and his features became smooth and friendly as he asked, "What's up, fellas?"

"The Father wants you to report in the throne room, Sir," Michael responded. He felt a little irritated at himself for feeling like a private in the presence of his drill sergeant.

"Then let's not keep Him waiting," Lucifer said with a smile and a tightening of his cherubic wings to his back.

As they strolled along, the three chatted like old friends. The two older angels couldn't help feeling a little guilty about any misgivings they might have been harboring.

When Lucifer's eye picked up the flaming trail, he stopped short. His gaze traveled its length as though trying to memorize it.

Turning to Gabriel, he stretched his arm out, pointing with his hand, palm up, and asked, "The final test?"

Gabriel grinned and answered, "Yes, don't step on that if you aren't pure in heart, but don't worry, you were created on such a high plane that you'll pass."

Gabriel frowned as they approached the throne room. Lucifer seemed a little ill at ease. "Probably this can be attributed to his being unaccustomed to the glory and splendor of the Holy of Holies," he thought. "And too, he hasn't had a chance to become used to being around anyone who outranks him, let alone to fellowship with the Creator."

Stepping through the veil, all three stopped short when struck by the glory which radiated from God, Himself. Love mingled with awe again spread across the faces of Michael and Gabriel. Awe, and was that not a touch of envy that Lucifer displayed?

The lion cherubim, for the first time since Michael and Gabriel had known them, displayed confusion. It was as if they were receiving conflicting messages from the Holy Spirit. Abruptly, their visages smoothed out and they extended their scepters to Lucifer as well as the two angels they were acquainted with.

"Welcome, My sons, and especially you, Lucifer, Star of the Morning. Come, let Us begin your education."

The lion-faced Cherubim held their scepters so they crossed over the heads of the three archangels as they passed them, and proceeded to the throne.

Lucifer joined in wholeheartedly. It appeared that love and loyalty were his two main characteristics. As a matter of fact, he would make full use of much of what he was learning in the not to distant future.

Certain phases he could have done without. He didn't care for standing at the throne with his wings sheltering it in his turn. This was boring and seemed to him to be rather beneath his dignity. You would not have detected any discontent; however, for he was much too good an actor for that. He did enjoy heading up the musical department for a short period of time. This too, however, seemed to him rather trivial for one with the assets he possessed.

God let him stew in his juices for a while, knowing all along what was in the angel's heart. Then calling Gabriel to his side, He asked, "Would you like a look at the plans We have for the future?"

Gabriel fairly beamed, and before he could answer, God continued, "All right, go find that wandering pal of yours. He'll want to hear too. You guys can sit in while I instruct Lucifer as to his part in the plans We have for creation."

Gabriel looked surprised, and then replied, "But Lord, I thought Lucifer was the end of Your creation."

"Ah, Gabriel, I said Lucifer was the end of the creation of angels. You, like many who will follow, tend to put meaning into My words that are not implied. Sometimes, you don't even hear all I say.

"It is true, there will be no more angels created, but there is much creation left. In fact, it really hasn't even begun. Now go get Michael so we can proceed."

Gabriel burst out of the Holy Place into the Outer Court like he was fleeing for his life. There was a portly little angel bent over watering some exotic flowers growing at the base of the gate post. He found himself in a knee, chest, and chin position, looking through the bush. A flower formed a floral mustache and tickled his nose.

Gabriel stopped and picked him up. "Oh, I'm really sorry, Posy." He brushed him off, and then left him standing there perplexed and sneezing.

Normally, Michael would have been one of the easiest angels in Heaven to find. It seemed to Gabriel, however, that he had just simply ceased to exist. When he did find him, he was in one of the wilder portions of the realm, drilling a legion of Heaven's crack warrior angels.

Gabriel rushed up panting. "Release the troops, pal. God has a treat for us like you never dreamed of and can't even imagine. Come on, I'll fill you in on the way back."

They had been trotting along for a while when Michael said, "Hey buddy, slow down a bit. You promised to tell me about this treat on the way back."

Gabriel slowed up enough to talk, but still didn't tarry. "Oh, forgive me, pal, God is going to instruct Lucifer concerning the future and his part in it, and He said we could sit in."

Michael was interested, but asked, "So What? What's so great about that?"

Gabriel actually took time to stop, and throwing his arms wide, exclaimed, "Buddy of mine, creation is over for angels, but God says that creation has really not even begun. Lucifer has some kind of part in this future creation, and we are going to get a first hand description of it. Is that worth hurrying for?"

Michael grinned at his excited friend, "Gabe, will you get out of my way? You sedentary types never could keep up with a soldier!"

Both friends laughed at each other, and turned to run together.

As they raced into the Outer Court, there stood Posy, whom Gabriel had run into on the way out. And this time, he was standing right in the center of the gate.

He started to turn left, and saw Gabriel bearing down on him, then right, and there was Michael. With a look of resignation, he stood stock still with his eyes closed. With merely a swish of air, the two mighty Archangels sped by him.

Now he just stood there bewildered that he was still standing and untouched.

They broke into the throne room just as the watch was changing. Momentarily, they forgot what they had even come for. Lucifer was one of the covering cherubim being relieved; and the choir was playing and singing one of his new compositions. The music was so beautiful that it sent a chill up their spines, and raised goose pimples on their flesh.

The two guardian cherubim at the throne raised their wings until they stood straight up, then with military precision, they took three steps back in unison. Their wings were then brought down in a motion similar to flight until they were horizontal, and then folded smartly to their backs. They then made right and left turns respectively until both faced forward beside the throne.

At a cue in the music, they stepped out in perfect thirty inch strides and took seven steps forward. The eighth[8] step relieved them from duty. Two cherubim stepped up, and again in perfect time to the music, reversed the procedure. They ended up with their wings touching over the Mercy Seat and the head of God. Thus, they formed a feathered canopy over the magnificent gem stone throne.

Lucifer greeted the other two high-ranking angels cordially, and with seeming sincerity as he turned on the personality. "Well fellows, are you ready to take a trip into the future with me?"

They could not help warming to the handsome angel leader. Michael answered enthusiastically, "You bet, we're all packed and ready to march, fly, or crawl; whichever or whatever happens to be the mode of travel."

They were grinning and joking, but dead serious in their determination not to miss a thing.

Lucifer stretched out a wing to get the kinks out of it, and said with a grin, "In a way, you guys are lucky you aren't cherubim. You don't have wings so you don't have to stand there for hours holding them over the throne."

Gabriel turned dead serious as he answered, "I would do anything God wanted me to do and do it gladly."

Lucifer went totally expressionless. "Oh sure, I would too."

At that moment, one of the angel choir stepped out and lifted a great, golden ram's horn. He blew a blast that re-echoed throughout the Mountain of God.

Lucifer turned all smiles. "Well, boys, there goes the school horn. Grab your slates and let's go."

They approached the throne with bowed head and dropped to their knees. God looked upon them smilingly and said, "Relax fellas, go ahead and make yourselves comfortable where you are. This will take a little time."

Each of them took a reclining position that suited them in the inches deep golden carpet. When all was quiet, the Lord proceeded, "What I am going to make known to you would not be within your powers of comprehension if I simply told you My plans. Consequently, We will show you what is to be."

Effortlessly, two mighty angels set a huge polished gem quality stone in position to form a TV like screen.

As the Lord began to speak again, the face of the screen turned so dark that the darkness itself, seemed to have depth. "What you are seeing, My children, is outer space. You tend to think in terms of the realm of Heaven. Since that is all you know, that is natural. However, outside our borders is an expanse of nothingness so large that you can't even begin to grasp its size.

"We have projected the present upon the screen. From now on, you will be seeing the future, as planned. At least, this is the perfect plan. There will be deviations as the need arises, but we will not go into that now."

A tiny spot of light appeared in the center of the screen and began to grow. "This is raw matter," Jehovah continued, "We will create it where nothing existed before and out of nothing."

The spot began to grow and become brighter. Its brightness was enhanced by the total darkness around it. Since it was in a complete vacuum, the eye traveled from extreme brightness to total darkness, enhancing the contrast.

The spellbound angels watched in awe as the Lord continued. "This is what you will see when the command to create is given—well not quite. This is a close up of what will occur a great distance from here." Even Lucifer seemed impressed.

The brilliant spot had reached such huge proportions that it seemed to take up the whole center of the screen. It now became obvious that the light came from a boiling, seething, superheated mass of matter.

The brightness reached a point well beyond that which human eye could have watched no matter how well protected. Now the angels even started showing distress. Just when it seemed they could stand it no longer—darkness! The blob's gravity was so great that light couldn't escape. Now it began to fall in within itself until its gravity reduced it to a tiny speck in space. The speck, however, was as heavy as the original mass had been. Then there was a roar that seemed to even shake Heaven as God added sound effects to make the exploding blob's image more authentic.

"There will be quite a long period of time while the mass of matter builds up, and between when it becomes dark and the explosion. We've speeded all the phases up for instruction time's sake," Jehovah said.

Instinctively, the angels had closed their eyes. Now as they opened them, they found themselves watching the greatest fireworks display ever set off.

The huge mass of matter had exploded. Now, smaller amounts of matter were streaking through the universe at unimaginable speed. At God's command, the new born stars and planets assumed their orbits, and the universe was born.

Now the scene changed as the image narrowed and seemed to zoom in on one spinning blob of white-hot elements.

Once more, Jehovah spoke to the watching angels, "This planet will be called Earth. It will be a special creation designed to support life. Even though the entire universe will be the realm of the angels, this planet is where you, Lucifer, will be stationed and carry on your ministry. At least to start with, creation on this planet will be in stages. Again, We have speeded up the processes in this display so you can see them in a short period of time."

The color of the great orb began to darken, and God went on to tell them, "This phase will be the longest of all. As creation proceeds, each phase will shorten and accelerate."

The three watched entranced as the colors changed from almost white to darker shades of red. As it reached this point, different shades of green and blue erupted from craters that appeared like those in boiling pudding. Next, a film like the scum on cold gravy began to appear. It was broken here and there by violent volcanic eruptions.

As though a video had been fast forwarded, they found themselves looking at an Earth that had a thin rind which shook and smoked. Steam spurted from cracks, and the air was full of the rumble of still more eruptions.

At last, it began to resemble a planet. It was still primitive, but volcanic mountains smoked and rumbled. Depressions began to appear, and there were clouds in the primitive atmosphere. Vicious lightening crackled from cloud to cloud and to the steaming earth.

Again, the image was fast forwarded. An Earth divided up into continents with small seas and full-fledged mountains cut by rivers came into view. Before their very eyes, it began to green up. The thick, smoky atmosphere began to clear and stars as well as a sun and moon began to appear.

God had just been letting them watch the panoramic view for a while. Now He spoke up again. "Up to this point, there will be no need for personal supervision on Earth. From now on, however, Lucifer goes to work. We are about to put animal life on the planet, and supervision will be needed. There will have to be laws. You might call them natural laws, but they originate right here. We make them!

Green appeared on the continents. Trees! Grass! Moss! Flowers—true plant life!

"You are about to see the first phase of the creation of animal life."

Abruptly, the waters fairly teemed with life. From nothing to highly complex types appeared before their eyes.

"The Earth will still be too primitive to support higher forms of life, so this period will continue for a time."

Once again, the camera seemed to leap ahead. Suddenly, they found themselves viewing Earth with not only birds and fish, but creeping reptiles, amphibians and dinosaurs. Again they were highly complex and created just as they stood. The next phase would bring warm-blooded animals, including primitive primates. Lucifer seemed mildly interested in these for a time. However, he was mainly thinking of the grandeur of being the mighty ruler of this Earth. He wondered if he could in any way duplicate the grandeur of God's throne room. How he would like to sit on a throne in that kind of setting.

Then came a phase which brought Michael and Gabriel up in excitement. Lucifer had a momentary attention lapse again as his thoughts were still on being the sole ruler of his own planet. He would be the king, virtually the god of this planet! Later, his recollections of this part wouldn't be nearly as clear as he might have wished. Not only were there warm blooded animals, but highly complex primates, including Cro-Magnon man and the likes of him.

When the excitement died down a little, God began to speak again, "With these creatures, your work will really begin, Lucifer. You will be expected to act as mediator and priest for them. You will instruct them in the worship of God."

"Yes," thought Lucifer, "and respect and deference to me."

Lastly, the camera seemed to pick up the Garden of Eden, and Adam and Eve. Again, a Lucifer who was somewhat bored, let his mind wander back to being all powerful upon this planet.

God spoke with loving pride now, "Here, you see the high point of creation on Earth. This creature is a three-part being just as We in the Godhead are—having body, soul, and spirit. He will be created in the image of God. His soul will be created similar to Our Holy Spirit. His spirit will be created similar to The Father, and his body will be created similar to Me, Jehovah—The Son. I will also, be known as The Angel of the Lord for many years. As the Son, I will be known as Jesus. Man will be created, literally, in Our image, you might say the first one will look just like Me. When you have assisted him to completion, he will be a higher creation than, and outrank all angels[9].

Lucifer came back to the present with a bump at this point. He had been selfishly, thinking so much about this coming experience, about being a king and a priest and all the power and glory that entailed, that he hadn't been paying enough attention. God's last statement brought him back to reality with a jolt. The thought was so repulsive to him that he couldn't even bring himself to look at this being which was to outrank him. Now he was devastated. All enjoyment drained from his face. It was bad enough to be outranked by God. This itself, was very distasteful to him, but a whole race of beings? Not only that, he was to help them attain this? He would have to give this some thought!

The lesson was over, and the crystal screen went dead. "Lucifer, I'm going to let you have a little time to yourself. You will need a good deal of help in your assignment on Earth. Why don't you start studying the angels to see which ones you think will suit you the best?" suggested God. "You have plenty of time, but you are going to need many angels to do the job properly."

It taxed Lucifer's very being to act natural, but he succeeded. "Yes, I believe that is a good idea."

When dismissed, he managed to leave without any show of haste, though his heart was raging within him.

CHAPTER III

THE CALLING OF THE CONSPIRATORS

After leaving the outer court, Lucifer walked aimlessly. He saw no one and responded to no one. His mind was turned completely into himself and his troubled, selfish thoughts. The glory he would have in this new position spelt nothing to him if he had to share it.

Gradually, as he walked, his mind turned from consternation and bewilderment to a cold seething fury.

Coming around a bend in a trail in a densely wooded area, he came face to face with another large, powerful angel whom he had never met before. Gone was diplomacy. Lucifer was in no mood to trifle with anyone.

Through clenched teeth, he ordered, "Get out of the way!"

The other angel didn't heed the danger signs and growled, "Apollyon steps aside for no angel or creature. Get out of the way, yourself!"

Though he had never needed to use them before, and probably never should have, Lucifer had built in knowledge of the martial arts befitting one who was a guardian of the throne. His movement was deft and surgical. It was so swift that Apollyon would never really know what happened. Suddenly, he found himself with his face driven into the ground and his body securely pinned.

For the first time in the big angel's life, he knew what stark terror was. He knew that he and Lucifer were on the ragged edge of what was lawful in Heaven by both their attitudes and their actions. Thus, he did not know how much further Lucifer was prepared to go.

Stones were trying to force their way into his mouth, but when one is desperate, anything is possible. Apollyon spoke around them.

"Mercy, Great Lucifer! I will never give you any trouble again!"

Lucifer arose, releasing Apollyon as he did so. With a devilish glitter in his black eyes, he repeated, "Get out of the way!"

Apollyon crab walked off the trail without even taking time to stand. He was actually thankful for the opportunity to do so.

Lucifer found himself feeling elated after the physical encounter. That was what he needed, a chance to excel! Also, the sight of the mighty Apollyon groveling at his feet almost had him feeling like his old self again. Then his mind went back to a whole race of people—Earthlings, would you believe—becoming higher than he, himself, and even outranking him. This caused him to grit his teeth anew.

Lounging in the shade by a roadside spring, Beelzebub and a group of his hangers-on were doing nothing in particular. Looking up the road, they saw Lucifer striding toward them.

Beelzebub squeaked, "Oh brother! Here comes our latest Great Angel. I'm sick and tired of Great Angels. Really, they aren't any greater or better than the rest of us. What if we don't show them all the respect they think they have coming? I'm sure God wouldn't allow them to do anything that would cause us too much discomfort. I'm going to test this old boy's air!"

Lucifer pulled abreast of them, still preoccupied with his own thoughts. Beelzebub gained his attention by snickering, "Lucifer the Great! What's it like at the top, Lucy?"

In a flash, Lucifer had a double handful of Beelzebub's robe right under his chin. Without even shortening his stride, he picked the little angel up bodily with one hand, grasped him by the ankle with the other hand, and stuck him head-first into the spring clear up to his waist. Lucifer held him there until the stream of bubbles began to thin down. One vicious glance at the others was enough to relieve them of any thoughts of valor they might have been entertaining.

Lucifer left Beelzebub under as long as he thought he dared. In a move that seemed effortless, he then raised him straight up, head down, sputtering and choking. Again, effortlessly, Lucifer turned him over like a baton until they were face to face.

Beelzebub's friends giggled in spite of themselves. His thin, scraggly hair was plastered on his head like a wet mop, exposing a round red, bold spot squarely on top of his head. His robe, now entirely soaked, clung to his pudgy little frame. It clung to him far enough up his body to show his skinny, chicken legs below his peaked, flat little hips, which were covered by his ragged undergarments. This robbed him of any dignity he might have ever had.

For a fleeting moment, a slight look of indignation started to cross his features. However, at that same moment, he caught Lucifer's eye. The look there left him able to fully sympathize with Apollyon. The same stark terror gripped his soul, and Beelzebub did not even have the courage to beg. A few watery blubbers escaped his stuttering lips.

Lucifer's expression changed to disgust. While holding him at arm's length, he simply opened his hands, and dropped the little angel like a wet rag. With a sneer on his face, he walked on.

"Oh no!" whispered an angel with large blue bags under his eyes. "Get ready for at least three hours of blusters and threats after he gets far enough away for it to be safe."

"Yah, we all know Beelzebub," answered a guy whose robe hung on him like a pair of droopy pants.

It was, however, a strangely quiet Beelzebub who picked himself up gingerly. He absently brushed his soggy hair out of his face, and sagged to a flat stone by the roadside.

"Air ya gonna get even with 'im?" asked a tall, skinny individual with buckteeth.

Beelzebub had a strange look on his face as he replied, "Fella, you are out of your mind! I am going to do my best to be one of his closest friends, if he has any. If he hasn't got any, I'll be his loyal servant."

A weasel faced character's nose almost seemed to quiver as he asked, "You mean you like him after what he did to you?"

"No, I'm afraid of him. Cross him too many times, and you could wake up dead. That is, if we can die. I sure wouldn't sell him short anywhere. If we can't be destroyed, he could make us wish we could. I'm sure he could reduce us to a formless spirit, which, I guess, is what death is. I don't think 'like' is going to be a word he understands for anyone except himself."

Baggy Eyes shook his head in wonder. "Boy, you sure sound different now than you did a few minutes ah-go."

Beelzebub brushed away a trickle of dirty water, which had run down his nose from his unwashed hair. "As the saying goes, 'I have seen the light'."

"Yes," said Weasel Face, "I can see what Beelzebub means; and this is hot off the press. I just heard it about an hour ago. I hear Lucifer is going to be recruiting quite a number of angels for some project or other. At least, that's what a warrior angel out of Michael's First Legion was telling me. He said Michael was called in to hear the orders given. It has to be big."

A cunning look crossed Beelzebub's face. "Lucifer doesn't seem too happy about something. You don't suppose he didn't like his orders, do you?"

Bucktooth was trying to keep up with the shifty minded Beelzebub, but without a great deal of success. Frowning in concentration, he lisped, "If'n he has 'is orders, he'll have to obey 'em whether he likes 'em or not, won't he?"

With a condescending look, Beelzebub crooned, "Will he now?" —leaving poor old Bucktooth as baffled as ever.

As Lucifer walked along, his mind kept jumping back and forth from God's plan, which he had already grown to hate, to his own turbulent thoughts. He relished his experiences with Apollyon and Beelzebub.

At least, he would have power in his new position. He had tasted raw power now, and liked the flavor. He could hurt people, and he liked that too! "I should be able to use this power in my new job," he thought. "If I can stretch it as far as I did today, there will be some compensation." Fleetingly, he thought, "I might be able to use this power on the people." Very fleetingly, he thought, "I just might hinder their development a little."

His mind again, shifted back to Apollyon. He gloried in the ease with which he had been able to handle the mighty angel. As he was thinking of Apollyon's great strength and agility, his mind branched off on a new tack. This guy might come in handy in the future, if he handled him right.

Lucifer's conceit was such that he had no doubt that he could handle him correctly. "I'll just offer him power, and he will be my man," he mused.

Unconsciously at first, and then with more malice-a-forethought, he was beginning to plan for his own wants and desires rather than the will of God.

Yes, he would recruit Apollyon. This shouldn't be any great problem. The problem would be, how was he to know which of the rest of the angels would be loyal when he took up residence on Earth? He would probably have several thousands of years after the initial creation before he would need to have his troops together. With all the angels he would require, that wasn't going to be any too much time at best.

"Apollyon isn't going to be much help here," he thought, "because I've got an idea that he isn't too well liked. Who would know the more rebellious spirits in Heaven?"

"Beelzebub! Yetch! What a creep! I hate it, but Beelzebub is simply going to be necessary to my plans."

For the first time since the verbal bombshell in the Holy of Holies, Lucifer was beginning to have peace of mind. The decision to rebel had become a reality.

He saw Michael and Gabriel in the distance, but adroit

maneuvering allowed him to avoid them. He did not feel in the mood for this kind of diplomacy right now.

Several hours later, and too agitated to relax, he decided to circulate and see just how Apollyon and Beelzebub had reacted to the manhandling they had received.

When he ran into Apollyon, he was not far from where they first met, and seated on a ledge overlooking a deep canyon with multicolored walls. The big angel was looking without seeing, lost in his own troubled thoughts. Lucifer approached quietly. Apollyon did not even know he was there until he sat down beside him. Surprise followed by sullen fear crossed his features. This was a feeling he was unaccustomed to, and he didn't like it a bit.

"Relax, my friend. You caught me in a bad mood before. I'd kind of like to be friends. As a matter of fact, I have a position of authority in mind for you if you are interested."

Suspicion replaced fear as Apollyon asked cautiously, "What kind of position could you give me that would be worth anything with characters like Michael and Gabriel holding all the good ones?" Pausing for an instant, he continued, "— at least one that I would want?"

Lucifer nodded more to himself than to Apollyon. "This guy isn't dumb even if he is muscle-bound," he thought.

"All right," Lucifer said, "the news is just out, so you may or may not have heard the latest. God is going to create new types of life. This won't be here. It will be on a planet, which He will also create. Never mind what a planet is. I don't think I could describe it so you could get the picture. What is important is that it will be a tremendous distance from here.

"In a sense, I will take the place of God there. I will need someone to act in the same capacity as Michael does here; for I will have a good portion of the angels of Heaven to help me to handle it."

Lucifer had chosen his approach well, and knew it as he watched the change of expressions come and go on Apollyon's face. Suspicion faded into comprehension. Hope and doubt followed simultaneously, and blended into excitement and acceptance.

The thought of having thousands of angels at his command simply bought his soul. Apollyon was ready to go to any length to attain this goal. He would follow Lucifer to Hell if necessary to reach it.

Lucifer had been careful not to say or set forth anything that would get him into trouble if it were repeated. In fact, anything Apollyon might say would only bring angels interested in going to Earth to Lucifer. This would give him a chance to start screening them right away.

Who would be the first one to apply? Beelzebub! Apollyon, Lucifer could, to a certain extent, relate to. Beelzebub was another matter. Lucifer was already learning that the path of unrighteousness is rough. He needed followers who were capable of evil, and evil comes in polluted containers. Even though he knew he would have to have Beelzebub's allegiance, he could not bring himself to go in search of the pudgy angel.

Hence, it was with relief mingled with regret that he saw the little fellow approaching after the equivalent of several days.

Beelzebub's own feelings were mixed. He held off coming to Lucifer after hearing that he had come to Apollyon. He hoped that he would be next. When Lucifer didn't come, Beelzebub swallowed his pride. Boy! That sure seemed to be on the menu quite often these days! Finally, he set out in search of the angel leader.

Beelzebub came cringing up to him rather like a whipped cur. Lucifer ignored him for a time, letting him writhe and grovel. He actually enjoyed the little angel's discomfort.

"Sir, I'm awful sorry for what I said back by the spring. I don't know how I could have been so stupid. If you'll just let me go to Earth with you, I'll do anything you want me to, so moot it be."

Finally, Lucifer seemed to notice him for the first time. Looking him right in the eye, which caused him to cringe even more, he said, "I'll make you a deal. If you can carry out this order, you can come. In fact, you will be something like Gabriel is here if you can do a good enough job."

The shock treatment had its effect. From not even knowing whether he could come or not to an offer of a princedom left even the sharp witted Beelzebub's mind a blank, momentarily.

When he caught his breath, he squeaked, "Oh Master, just name it!"

That "Oh Master" cinched it for Beelzebub. Lucifer might not ever really like the little guy, but he certainly thrived on this kind of balm to his spirit. Yes, he would have to keep him around.

"All right," he continued, "I need someone to recruit angels who will be completely loyal to me in any circumstances for Project Earth. Avoid any that already have positions of authority here. Your job is simply to recruit, and recruit well. Find those who aren't satisfied; who think they have been short changed. Find those who are hungry for more power, prestige, and rank. I want guys who will take my orders without question or thought. In other words, guys that have or think they have something to gain."

Beelzebub's expression had turned shrewd and calculating. "Yah, I know a whole bunch of guys that would fit that description. Master, am I to understand that these orders are strictly yours?"

With a look that sent him shrinking back again, Lucifer spoke slowly and with emphasis, "Beelzebub, too much knowledge could destroy you!"

Beelzebub stammered, "Yes Sir! Oh, yes Sir! I'm sure it could; and no smarter than I am, I sure don't know anything!"

Lucifer grinned coldly, but not unkindly, "You bet. That's why I've given you as big an assignment as I have."

The left-handed compliment left Beelzebub feeling a little better. When Lucifer continued, he had his servant's undivided attention.

"Now when you are absolutely sure of your angel, bring him to me. I will make the final decision. If I don't think I can mold him to my will completely, I will reject him.

"If you have any friends that you feel can help you without getting tangled up with the wrong 'people', bring them to me. I'll visit with them at length. If I think they're all right, you can have them bring their recruits to you. These guys should be character judges that will know whether I would want an individual or not, and that is all. Understand? Maybe the ones who were with you at the spring?"

"Yes, Master," responded Beelzebub, who had shrewdly deduced how much Lucifer liked the term. "But you don't want any of those guys for anything that is important. I do know some who should work out well, however. Anything more?"

"No, not at the present, anyway. By the time your men have screened them, then you have, followed by my final inspection, we should have a pretty loyal crew. You are dismissed."

If Beelzebub resented the abrupt dismissal, he gave no sign of it.

Lucifer could not have cared less what Beelzebub thought. He'd had all of the little creep he could stand.

CHAPTER IV

CREATION

Again, the word was being carried throughout the realm. Another step in creation was about to be taken. This time, no one would have to gather for no matter where they were, they would be able to see as much as there was to see.

God was about to create the universe. What they were to see would not be nearly as spectacular as what the three mighty angels in the Holy of Holies saw. They had been privileged to see close up what now would be seen at an uncomprehendible distance.

Since God was the light of Heaven, the sky, itself, was inky black. There were no sun, moon, or stars so the angels with the exception of the three Archangels had no concept of what to expect.

In spite of the fact that God warned that for a while, they might not be able to see a great deal, and when they could, it wouldn't be much for the equivalent of several years, all were standing staring into the blackened heavens when the command went forth.

For a few moments, it did, indeed, seem that nothing had happened. Then, a tiny pinpoint of light was seen glowing faintly in the sky. It grew in brightness for the equivalent of millennia. Now, even at the great distance, it was brighter than any modern star.

We would have been unimpressed, but to angels who had

never seen a star, it was in fact spectacular. Every so often, someone could be seen standing staring into the heavens.

It grew in intensity until it was easily visible. Finally one day, the spellbound Baggy Eyes asked, "What is it going to do now?"

"It's going to explode," answered Droopy Drawers.

"What's explode?" asked Bucktooth

Droopy Drawers looked down his nose disdainfully at Bucktooth for a moment and then his expression went blank.

"He don't know either," said Weasel Face with a squeak that was as near a laugh as he could muster.

Baggy Eyes looked down, rubbing his watering eyes, and said, "None of us really knows anything about this. We're just going to have to wait and see what happens."

Even as Baggy Eyes spoke, Bucktooth exclaimed "Look! It's gone!"

For a long period of time, all was blackness, then one day—"There's the light! It's back!" squeaked Weasel Face, who had just happened to look up. "The light's back, and it's gettin' bigger and brighter!"

Even as the motley group watched, it seemed to turn into a mist and slowly grow larger and dimmer.

"I-It's-slowin' down," stammered a nervous angel with a twitch.

"Yah, and I'm gettin' bored and hungry. I'm goin' to go find something to eat," added a short, fat little angel.

When all the excitement had died down, Gabriel turned to Michael, and remarked, "I have a couple questions I want to ask the Father. I'll see you around."

"Not so fast, old buddy, you have a lot more time with the Father than I do. Consequently, you ask for answers that I don't even know the questions to. And, I've got a hunch this is going to be interesting. No Sir! You can't get rid of me that easy, Pal!"

Gabriel laughed and slapped Michael on the shoulder. "OK, yet, be my guest."

Beastie and Creature met them affectionately as the two

friends stepped through the veil. The lion heads were smiling on their human side as they extended their scepters. Beastie's Lion face was purring, and he rubbed against Michael like an oversized pussy cat. Michael vaulted over his back like a boy jumping the yard fence in a vain attempt to get away, laughing all the while.

Finally, the two large creatures settled down. Michael wiped his brow and remarked to them in mock sternness, "I'm sure glad you guys aren't any bigger."

Beastie's human face chuckled. Michael was one of his few chances for exercise, and he knew Michael enjoyed their romps as much as he. He was also sure that the Father enjoyed the byplay as much as they did.

The two Archangels dropped to their knees at the throne and were joined by the two seraphim and their regal cherubim friends. After a short praise service with all enveloped by the almost tangible love of the Father, Jehovah asked, "What's on your minds, fellas?"

Gabriel spoke up, "Well, Father, I have a couple questions, and even though Michael doesn't know what they are, he thought he needed to know the answers, too."

At this, both creatures laughed right out loud, and Michael even had to chuckle.

"Well, Gabriel, I see you are still learning. It isn't often anymore that you have to ask questions. What is troubling you?"

"I'm not really troubled, Father, but as you have taught us, light travels at a given rate of speed. How is it that we were able to see the light from the great mass of matter so soon, even though it was so terrifically far away?"

"Ah, Gabriel, you have learned your lessons well. Yes, it would have taken light many years to reach us if we had only created the matter. However, We are not limited to merely creating matter. When we created the matter, we also created the rays of light that reached from it to us. Now let Me go further, and so eliminate the need for your next question. You were able to see the explosion as it occurred, simply because We wished to let you observe it. We accelerated the creation time so that in a much shorter time, We did what otherwise would have taken a very long period. We can, and at times will, bend our own natural laws. And, yes, the matter grew, fell in upon itself, and exploded at an accelerated rate. Again, simply because We wished to do it that way."

"Thank You, Lord. After You explain it, it seems so simple."

"Don't be troubled, Gabriel, there will come a time when this same question will deceive literally millions of those on Earth. But that is enough of this line of thinking. You will be asking questions that I am not at liberty to answer at this time."

Gabriel, indeed, would have liked to ask some more questions now, but knew that the subject was closed. He contented himself with the knowledge that God had said, "At this time." That meant that sometime his questions would be answered. That had to suffice.

As they were turning to leave, Michael laid his hand on Creature, and asked, "Where are the rest of your buddies? I haven't seen them for some time. You're operating at about a fourth capacity lately, aren't you?"

"Yes," replied Creature. "We're running in shifts now, because it seems that when 'Operation Earth' gets under way, there won't be much rest for us. Us four, and Rex, Taurus, Manny, and Eagle will virtually go nonstop for several thousands of years. We haven't had our rest and recreation break yet, but shortly, Lovable and Sweet Thing will be relieving us.

"Your whole ministry is praise and worship. Will that be such a big deal?" asked Gabriel. "In a way, it's like you guys are the pets of God."

Creature's human face grinned knowingly. "Yes, its kind of like we have been big pussy cats on the hearth, up until now, that is. But God didn't create us just for that. You might say we are the crew that runs the ship."

"Ship?" asked Michael, "What are you talking about?"

Creature looked a little smug, but the knowledge within

him, which for once, these two mighty angels didn't know, was bursting to come out.

"Look around you," he said with something of an air. "You think you see it all, but let me tell you, you haven't seen the half of it."

Both mighty angels looked skeptical, but remained silent.

Creature continued, "Beneath the floor, there is a huge brazen altar and gigantic wheels within wheels. The altar is banked now; however, the fire that seems to be in the floor comes from it, and actually is under the floor. For some reason, at some time during Operation Earth, the altar won't be banked. I don't really understand it all, myself, But God says that sacrifice will be what powers it. We'll take up positions on all four sides of it. We literally drive it when God wants to go to Earth—that is, when the entire Godhead wants to go as one.

"You know how God the Holy Spirit is everywhere, much like the air is. He can be sitting on the throne as one third of the Godhead, while being in His seven parts in the lamps at the same time. Jehovah—Jesus—the body of the Godhead by whatever name you want to call Him—can be everywhere, but He doesn't do that so often. The Father can be too, but very seldom is anywhere but on the throne. This way, They can go wherever they want as the one Triune God, and never leave the throne."

"Are you going to give us a ride?" Michael asked with a grin.

"Oh, I'm sure God would give you guys a ride. In fact, I'm sure it will be necessary at times."

"Well, I'd guess that will be a long time from now," Gabriel said. "In the mean time, you are ready for a vacation, Huh?"

"Oh, we've got it all planned. We're going to run and jump and fly through every forest and off every hill in Heaven when we get the chance. —and anyway, we'll be trading off with Manny, Eagle, and those guys after Operation Earth begins. God gives everyone a break once in a while. We will have two full crews so we'll always have one resting."

In his enthusiasm over his vacation, Creature actually

jumped up and down, spreading his four great wings. Michael ducked and headed for the veil and safety.

At God's accelerated rate of creation, the universe was getting to be more than just a tiny spot of mist. It still had the appearance of a mist of light; however, it covered most of the heavens now. Individual pinpoints of light were beginning to be seen as some of the larger and brighter stars got close enough to be visible.

In the mean time, Lucifer's task of recruitment was proceeding admirably. Beelzebub was proving himself very apt at his job, and even winning the grudging admiration of his master. However, Lucifer would have died rather than let the little drip know it.

Michael was hurrying along on an administrative mission, when, with a thunder of mighty wings, the beautiful six winged seraphim, Rex, Taurus, Manny, and Eagle came to rest around him. The look of consternation on his face sent them into gales of laughter. Michael joined in after he caught his breath.

When the laughter subsided, Michael asked, "How are you guys enjoying your vacation?"

They all started to speak at once, then all stopped and started over again, one at a time.

The lion headed Rex said, "I love the jungle, Michael. You can slip through it without making a sound."

The bull headed Taurus shook his head, "I don't like that at all. I would rather roam around out in the meadows."

Eagle turned his snow-white bald eagle head so he was looking at Michael with one piercing eye, and remarked, "I don't know why anyone would want to stay anywhere down here, when you can soar so high and watch what is going on everywhere. There is simply nothing like feeling the wind in your face."

Manny's tastes were more varied, and he rather liked it all. At the mention of watching the activities below, he sobered and a worried expression crossed his handsome human like features.

He began with a certain intensity, "Michael, we are in ah

unique situation. Most of the angels don't take us seriously, and speak freely around us. It appears that Lucifer is recruiting strictly out of the ranks of the maladjusted, discontented, and power hungry. Apollyon and Beelzebub are his top lieutenants, which should tell you something.

Shock went through Michael in waves as the import of Manny's statement began to sink in.

"Excuse me, fellas, I've an important mission to fulfil, and then, I must get to the Father and find out what the meaning of all this is," he said, spinning on his heel. Gone was the side of Michael that was friendly, likeable, and fun loving. The angel who strode away was Michael, Commander-in-chief of the Armed Forces of Heaven!

Later, when his mind was more at ease, he would think to apologize to his four friends for the abrupt way in which he had terminated the conversation.

As a matter of fact, even though Michael's reaction tended to confirm their worst fears, it was a relief to know that the mighty Michael was about to do something. They understood his reactions completely.

For the first time that anyone could remember, Michael did not pause to absorb the beauty as he entered the veil, but ran to the throne and threw himself prone at the feet of the Father. For a few moments, he was so shaken he couldn't even speak.

Gabriel, standing at the side of the throne, and knowing his friend as he did, knew that something approaching a disaster must have struck. Protocol, however, forbade him to speak in this kind of situation. He did not have long to wait, though, as the Father said, "Easy Michael. What's the matter?"

Michael sat up, gazed imploringly at the Father, and began: "Father—what is Lucifer doing? He has recruited Apollyon and Beelzebub as his lieutenants. He is putting together a crew of rebels. What does this mean?"

Glancing aside at Gabriel, Michael, under any other circumstances, would have had to laugh. Gabriel's expression gave one the impression that he had just been kicked in the stomach, and had not gotten his breath back yet. Now, however, there was no humor in anything for Michael.

"Ah, Michael, indeed, you do your job well. It surely didn't take you long to be up on the situation. Yes, My children, there is sin in the kingdom."

Michael, the typical soldier, immediately responded, "Father, let us stop them before they become any stronger. It is bad enough now, but if Lucifer gains many more followers, we will be looking at full scale angelic war. Father, the very thought of that is frightening and sickening!"

"Oh Michael, My impetuous child, We are not just thinking of military conquest. If we were, I would have had you and your fine troops stop Lucifer as soon as he made up his mind to sin."

Now that the talk had reached the informal stage, Gabriel spoke up, "Is it not true that now, we must think in terms of individuals as pertains to loyalty and disloyalty?"

"Yes, Gabriel, but it goes far beyond that. We must deal with sin itself. As you fellows noticed some time ago, many have been travelling on a thin line just as close to sin as they thought they dared. Sooner or later, they were bound to step over.

"Lucifer must be left to his devices so those who have the inclination will take their stand with him, and those who wish to remain true to Me will take theirs."

Michael, still the military man, was already thinking war and consequences. "After we have defeated them, You will imprison them in some way so that they can't corrupt anyone else. Spiritual death and separation will be their reward for eternity, right?"

"Not so fast, My fire breathing warrior, sin is not that easy to eradicate. We would see a replay of what happened here, among the humans on planet Earth shortly. We would have to go through this all over again.

"No, Lucifer must go there as planned. He will have a chance, while there, to save himself and his followers. As perfect beings, they have the power to live righteously and guide those who are there that way.

"Should they do this, they could redeem themselves. I may add. They will not make use of the opportunity. They will cause the fall of mankind—don't look at Me that way, My beloved Michael. Sure, I could turn you and your legions loose and stop them. Then what would happen? Humans of the ilk of Apollyon and Beelzebub would be falling throughout eternity. We would have an ever festering wound.

"This way, the humans who are inclined to, will go over to Lucifer just as the natural sinners did here. Mankind will go through a time period involving several thousands of years. All of the time, they will be following a plan that I have for them. When this time period is over, sin will be forever destroyed. Fallen men and angels alike will be judged, and reduced to one part beings. The one part of course is their spirits. Then they will be imprisoned in Hell for eternity."

Gabriel looked up, "Hell—?"

"Yes, Gabriel, Hell hasn't been created yet. It will be created for Lucifer and his angels. The sub-humans you saw in the preview will fall before it is created, and Lucifer will be able to use their spirits in his evil schemes. The true humans will be created afterward and the spirits of the fallen ones will go to Hell. The saved ones will go to Paradise, both awaiting judgment. That is enough for now. You will understand it better as you see it unfold.

"Remember now, you must not let on to Lucifer that you know anything is amiss," continued the Lord. "And Michael, don't drill the troops too hard. It will be several thousands of years before you do any fighting. You might do some training for spy operations, for it will do your troops good to see what is going on when the action really starts. After a certain point, many of you will have to do duty as guardian angels for those who choose to follow Me on Earth."

CHAPTER V

INFANT EARTH

Michael's eyes squinted, and his handsome, normally peaceful features were twisted into a frown. He shook his head as he spoke to Gabriel. "Since Earth is turning green, it seems like Lucifer is everywhere at once."

"Yah, it's sickening to see how happy and pleasant he acts. He's inspected everything at least two or three times."

"Uh-huh, he's certainly not leaving anything to chance."

Both were quiet for a while, and then Michael continued, "You know, it's almost going to be a relief not having to pretend that all is lovely and normal when you know what he is doing and going to do."

"Ah," Michael sighed, "it's finally, time to move."

Lucifer's angels stood on a vast plain. Michael shuddered a little as he looked out across the mighty throng. The next time he saw them thus, they would be in battle formation.

All was ready for transporting. God would not need any kind of 'Transporter Room', or any other science fiction type apparatus. His word would be quite sufficient. The entire host would be transported in an atomic portion of a second too small to ever be measured by any means—the speed of thought.

A hush fell over both groups of angels as Jehovah—Jesus Christ in His preincarnate flesh, appeared. The Shekinah cloud of the Father enveloped Him like a many colored robe of supernatural beauty.

Jehovah raised His hand and began to speak, "In the name of the only triune God, be removed to Earth!"

Instantly, the vast plain was empty. For a few moments, there was a total silence. It was as though none had the breath to speak, then a mighty cheer went up. These folks had seen many miracles, but to be this close to one of this magnitude was something else.

Beelzebub turned to Bucktooth and in breathless tones said, "If God can do that, what can't He do?"

One thing was instantly apparent. They were no longer in Heaven. The Earth they looked out across was very primitive, indeed.

There was a good deal of plant life, but even most of this was not very tall. The circumstances in most areas were really not right for many of the more advanced forms of plant life of the larger sort to thrive in.

Hot springs spurted steam in minieruptions, and volcanos welcomed them with the real thing.

Lucifer was the only one there who had any idea of what to expect. The rest viewed this foreign and rather hostile environment with a certain amount of concern if not consternation.

The area they sat down in would be called the District of Eden after the Eden in Heaven. Lucifer unrolled a huge scroll, and began to read to himself. After a few moments, he raised his eyes and said, "All right, our immediate orders are to set up the temple over which I will preside as priest and mediator for Earth's creatures."

Lucifer spread his wings, and lifted to a rock. With a flourish he turned to face the throng. His features now, were different than they had ever seen them in Heaven. They were harsh and cruel, perhaps even evil.

He had no intention of starting a full-fledged rebellion at present. That would come later, when he hoped he could move from a position of strength. Also, a golden, jewel encrusted temple in which he could strut and show off his equally jewel bedecked priestly garments was an order that he would not have any trouble complying with.

Unrolling the scroll, he looked at it briefly, then pointed to a smoking volcano in the distance. "That is the southwest corner of New Eden." Swinging his arm around, he added, "that pass in the mountain range is the southeast one." Again, turning some more and pointing down the valley, he said, "That little lake is the northwest corner and that funny bald mountain is the other corner. We are to acquaint ourselves with the area before we start anything. I've got the blueprint for the temple, and we will mark the area for it, first thing."

He set up his temporary field command post along the side of the temple site, and again began giving orders. "We are going to need a lot of raw materials. We'll give the leaders of the work crews lists of things to look for. We'll set up smelters for refining gold and other precious metals right away."

Mining crews soon were bringing in not only various kinds of metal ore, but uncut gem stones as well. Crews of artisans began cutting and polishing the stones.

In some of the more sheltered valleys, suitable timber was found. These were felled, trimmed, and brought in where they were sawn, hewed, and planed for use.

In time, the building itself began to rise, doomed to failure from the ground up. Again, there would be three parts. Outer court, Holy Place, and Lucifer in the Holy of Holies!

The temple reached completion, and without any dedication or sanctification, but merely a wild party, Lucifer moved in.

Back in Heaven, the Lord watched with aching heart. For the benefit of Michael and Gabriel, as well as Lovable and Sweet Thing, who had replaced Beastie and Creature, God again set up the beautiful gem stone screen. He also set one up in the outer court for any others who wished to watch.

Watching now became a duty done simply to keep informed. What should have been a time of rejoicing for the angels, now turned into a time of mourning. At times, Michael was all for attacking at once, such was his anguish.

"The time has come for us to create the first phase of life on Earth, fellas," said the Lord. "If you wish to watch."

This would be interesting, so all gathered around the crystal screen.

Meanwhile, on Earth, Bucktooth, Beelzebub's pal, hadn't changed at all. He had found an out of the way spot, overlooking a small lake. There he could hide out and avoid anything that might resemble work. For one thing, he couldn't seem to get anything right. This way, he could stay out of trouble.

At the Lord's command for the waters to bring forth life, old Bucktooth was staring into the water, his mind a blank as usual. A fish fully six feet long swam by. Typically, there was a time lag while Bucktooth's mind began to function. Suddenly, bang! It perked! With a shriek, he fell down without really getting up first. Then, he fell down twice more before he could get his knobby knees and oversize feet into action.

Doubtlessly, he would have been subject to disciplinary action the way he barged into the inner sanctum if he had not had such important news—and been so terror stricken.

The Lord zoomed in on Bucktooth and gave His faithful lieutenants a ring side seat to his consternation. By the time Bucktooth was lisping incoherently at Lucifer's feet, all the dignity of the two Archangels and creatures was gone. They were in a heap at the base of the screen, their arms around each other, and weak from spasms of racking laughter.

Lucifer, himself, was amused at the spectacle of this gawky court jester. He realized, however, that whatever had excited him to this extent had to be important. He spoke soothingly, "Easy, Pal. Unwind and tell me what you've found. What's the matter?"

When speech was again possible, Bucktooth gasped, "A wallopin' what's it—in the lake. It's big enough ta eat a guy, and it looks hungry!"

One moment, Bucktooth was the center of attention, and the next, he found himself talking to an empty room.

Lucifer, Beelzebub, Apollyon, Rege, and about a dozen

others who happened to be there, almost jammed the door in their haste to see for themselves if what Bucktooth said was true. Such was their excitement that they didn't even feel any resentment at being jostled.

Soon, reports of sightings of life in the waters were coming in from all over Eden. No doubt about it, the first step in the creation of life had been taken.

"I wonder why God didn't warn us first," mused Beelzebub.

"I thought about that," nodded Lucifer. "What it shows is just how much God trusts us. He didn't figure we needed any warning."

Without even turning his head to look at them, Lucifer ordered curtly, "Beelzebub and Apollyon, bring your lieutenants and meet me in the inner sanctum."

When all had gathered around the throne, Lucifer became dead serious.

"What you have seen today is just a very minute beginning. God will continue to create higher and more advanced forms of life. He intends to proceed until He creates 'Man'. This creature is supposed to reach a point at which he is a higher and more advanced being than we are, and will even outrank me. Needless to say, I am not going to allow this!"

Even bold Apollyon paled at this forthright assertion. He spoke just above a whisper, "Lord Lucifer, where God can even read our thoughts, is it safe to speak as you are?"

"Ah, my gullible friend, do you see me cast into some kind of Hell? As a matter of fact, if God could read my thoughts, I would have been roasting in flames somewhere ever since God told us Man would be above me. I began to wonder right then just how much that he told us was true.

"I don't doubt that He can blend His Spirit with the life of these creatures that he has just created. I don't doubt that He can cause them to follow any pattern of action that He wishes them to. However, I believe that by a process of mind control and extrasensory perception, we can override His influence."

"In a word, I don't think He's as big and powerful as He would have us to believe—and I intend to prove it!

"I, for one, don't want anyone, even God, to be above me. I hated that from the beginning. Now, we are going to start right in to see that they don't get there!" After a few moments of silence, almost musingly, he continued, "Yah, it was in the back of my mind that I didn't even want God above me before I found out that these people would be also."

Despite his keen intelligence, Beelzebub was puzzled. "Master, what can we do yet, to stop this man thing from being over us?"

Lucifer answered his creepy PR. man condescendingly, "Beelzebub, have you studied these water creatures?"

"Yes Sir," answered Beelzebub, "and I don't for the life of me, see what you can do yet, to thwart God's plans at this point."

"That's the reason you will never be really great in life, my friend," returned Lucifer unkindly, "and why you are not sitting where I am. Tell me, Prince Beelzebub, what do these creatures eat?"

With head down, unable to meet Lucifer's vicious gaze, Beelzebub mumbled, "They appear to eat moss and other water plants, as near as I can tell."

"Hurrah!" mocked Lucifer. Turning to Apollyon, and mellowing his approach somewhat, he asked, "How well do they get along, my warrior?"

"Remarkably well," Apollyon said, saying as little as possible.

"OK, we have two points of attack," Lucifer said, with a malicious glint in his eyes. "We will influence them by means of mental telepathy, and start them eating each other. Hatred, fear, and suspicion will naturally follow. Fighting will be the result. I detected microscopic life in the water. I believe we can even control that the same way.

"We will start out getting the microbes to eat each other. It will just be one more step getting them to attack the larger beasts. Then, you have sickness and death."

After a thoughtful pause, Lucifer continued, "Get your men together and practice mind control. Those who get the hang of it quickly can move right out. We will use this as sort of a training ground. From here, it is the whole world! We will blanket it completely!"

After further thought, Lucifer again continued, "Perhaps we should have a leaders' workshop, and I will demonstrate personally to you what I have in mind. Then you can train your lieutenants. They, in turn, can help you train the rank and file. In about an hour, meet me at Bucktooth's lake, and witness a miracle!"

When Lucifer strode up to the lake, he was pleased to see that he would be performing to a standing room only crowd. His followers stepped back, making him a path as he moved through them. His ego was so high when he reached the lake that he almost thought, himself, that he was God.

Sitting down about where Bucktooth had been when he had seen the first big fish, Lucifer placed his head in his hands, and became oblivious to all that was around him. He, with single-mindedness, was concentrating on the simple minds of the large fish in the lake.

"I-I-I w-w-wonder how l—ong we'll have t-ta wait," stuttered Nervous.

"Probably quite a while," Fat Boy answered, pessimistically.

This was to Lucifer's liking, however, for he could make a more spectacular showing this way.

"Look!" Weasel Face exclaimed. " They're here already!" Two large fish were swimming side by side, coming up to the bank where Lucifer was sitting. Upon approaching the bank, they circled, showing neither hostility nor friendship—simply ignoring each other, except to stay in formation.

Lucifer raised his head long enough to speak to the onlookers. "Watch closely, for I am about to override God's commands to these brutes."

Again, he dropped his head into his hands. The two great fish began to behave strangely. Their formation broke up, and they began to circle each another in opposite directions. Huge dorsal fins stood erect. Their swimming motions became jerky. The sleek bodies were held in ridged half circles. Heads and tails alike, were pointed at the opponent. With a savagery never before witnessed by the fallen angels, the mighty fish came together with nothing but murder in their primitive minds. Due to the depth of the water along the bank at the point where the fish were fighting, the only thing that clouded the water was air and bits and pieces of the fish.

Raising his head again, Lucifer spoke anew, "This is just the first step. Now watch step two." Once more, his head dropped into his hands. Abruptly, the water was full of hundreds of small fish. They came in response to Lucifer's bidding and the smell of blood in the water.

They darted about in a crazed frenzy. They slashed and snapped at anything that moved, including one another. Shortly, it was obvious that the two big fish had been eaten, and the small ones were still fighting amongst themselves in the bloody water. The water now, was so roiled that motion was all one could see.

Lucifer raised his head and stood to his feet. "This is an example of what you will be doing world wide. As soon as you have it mastered, you will be assigned spheres of influence."

Looking around, he met Bucktooth's uncomprehending stare, and continued, "In other words, you will be told where you will be working. Do you understand?"

Even Bucktooth nodded now, and Lucifer stalked away.

Apollyon had just pried his attention away from the boiling mass of fish. He fairly skipped around in his excitement. He could really get into something like this! Death held him in an almost hypnotic spell. Well was he named—Apollyon the Destroyer!

Apollyon was not the only warrior who was almost beside himself. Light years away, Michael was pacing in circles around the beautiful crystal screen. He was about as near raving as he had ever been. Gone was the fear and distaste for angelic war that he had felt earlier.

"Father, let me ruin this petty criminal! Build your prison. I'll stuff him in it, head first, through a window!"

Even as he spoke, he knew he had spoken amiss and dropped his head and moaned, "I'm sorry, Father, but oh, those beautiful creatures. He's destroying them just to further his own cause."

The Lord spoke quietly, "This is just the beginning, My beloved soldier. Wait until you watch him crucify Me, after having beaten Me beyond recognition. He will pull out all My hair, and whip the skin and flesh from My chest and back. Virtually every bone in My body will show somewhere."

Michael had stopped, one foot suspended in midair, In a voice barely above a whisper, he breathed, "You would let him do that, my God?"

"You've just had a small taste of what sin does by watching what is going on down there on Earth. That is the only way to completely rid the universe of it. The price is not too high to pay since it will rid us of the problem of sin forever. Simply stated: God must die for, or instead of, man."

Always thinking, even when grief stricken, Gabriel looked up and asked, "How can You die, Father? You are immortal."

"We planned this out long ago. In order to die, I will have to transform My body into half the DNA of an embryo in a woman's womb. I will have to grow up as a human being. This way, I will be God in a body that can die. I will still be sinless, and have all My powers as God. I will have to put up with the physical shortcomings of a mortal body so that I can die for man. My human name will be Jesus, which means savior."

Watching the grief-stricken angels, the Lord queried, "Would you fellas rather not be able to watch? We can remove the screen, you know. I placed it there strictly for your convenience."

Gabriel spoke up quickly, "Father, even if it brings grief, I must know what is going on. If you have given us a choice, that is."

The rest numbly nodded their agreement. They too, wished to know what was going on below.

"Cheer up, boys," added the Lord. "It will be several thousands of years before the crucifixion takes place. For the immediate future, he will take out his venom upon the fallen angels and My creatures that are entrusted to him."

On Earth, Lucifer's angels were practicing mind control like it was some new toy. For some, it came easy. They had a ball controlling the inhabitants of the lakes and streams. They even enjoyed training their fellow angels who hadn't caught on so quickly.

Beelzebub's sharp, twisted little mind caught on quickly, but, alas, Bucktooth! Finally getting a chance to speak to Beelzebub alone, Bucktooth confessed, "Beelzebub, ah jest cain't seem ta git mah mind clost ta one ah them thar fishes a-tall. Ya s'pose ya-all could give me a hand?"

Beelzebub looked doubtful. "Bucktooth, I'm not sure you've got the mind for it; but we'll give it a try."

Somehow, Bucktooth thought he had been complimented, and shambled off happily after Beelzebub. For one thing, if he didn't have the mind for it, he might not have to have anything to do with those big fishes. He just couldn't help it. They still frightened him.

Beelzebub sat down by the bank and Bucktooth sat down beside him. "Now Bucktooth, try to blend your mind with mine; and we will call a fish up to the shore. Just close your eyes and concentrate."

Beelzebub didn't know it, but he had blown it already. Bucktooth wasn't about to sit there on the bank, and shut his eyes; not with him knowing that a fish was going to swim up to them. "No, sir-ee Bob!" How could he hope to run if he had to open his eyes first?

Beelzebub had presence of mind enough to influence a small fish to come. When Bucktooth saw that it was a 'little teeny one', he shut his eyes and screwed up his face to such an extent that when Beelzebub opened his eyes, he thought, "Well, give him credit for effort, anyway."

"You can look now, Bucktooth."

Bucktooth opened his eyes as though he had been hard at it all the time, and was surprised that the fish was there already.

"All right, Bucktooth, concentrate on the fish's mind and think, 'turn around'."

Bucktooth tried, but when Beelzebub released the fish from

his own control, it darted away, Beelzebub then, had to bring it back. After repeating the process several times with the same result, Beelzebub gave up.

"Those fish just don't listen to you, Bucktooth, but don't feel bad, my friend. Do you remember Lucifer mentioning microscopic life? I'll bet you could handle them."

Bucktooth turned pale and stammered, "Air—air they as big as their name, Beelzebub?"

Beelzebub had to giggle before answering reassuringly, "No, old buddy, they are so small that you can't even see them. However, Lucifer wants them to eat each other, and maybe even the fish and other stuff in the lake."

Bucktooth let out a yell of pure delight and tried to turn a cartwheel. He landed on his head without even wiping the smile from his face. Even he wasn't afraid of something that small. Yah, and if it got rid of the fish, so much the better. Yes, he thought he could handle that!

Enough of the angels had ESP. under control to assign them their districts. Now reports were coming in rapidly.

The lieutenant's feet shuffled, and his head sagged. Boy, did he ever hate to give his report. "Lord Lucifer, uh, it seems that some species just simply won't eat flesh."

Lucifer's eyes flashed in anger. "What? What is the matter with you misfits? O-h-h-h for some decent help! If you goofs cause me to lose this war with God, whatever He has in mind for you will be mild to what I'll do to you!" After a pause, he continued in a somewhat quieter voice. "They'll all fight, though, won't they?"

"Yes, Sir," the trembling fallen angel answered quickly.

"Well, since I can't be everywhere at once, I guess that will have to do." In the back of his mind, the thought that God could, indeed, be everywhere, nagged him—at least, He said He could—Lucifer told himself he didn't believe it.

"Master, can I keep Bucktooth with me where I can keep an eye on him?" asked Beelzebub.

Lucifer didn't answer right away as he thought about it.

"Yah, I guess so. I really can't think of anyplace where I could send him if I wanted to."

To himself, he thought, "At least, I can stand old Bucktooth easier than I can Beelzebub. Bucktooth is good for a laugh or two. Goodness knows, those are hard enough to come up with around here. If I didn't need Beelzebub so much, I'd put him on the other side of the world."

Apollyon was in the height of his glory, traveling around the world, overseeing the worldwide attack on the new life forms. Murder, killing—in short, death the only thing on his mind.

CHAPTER VI

CREEPERS

It was Officers Call in the Holy Place on Earth. Lucifer looked thoughtful as he began to speak. "It has been long enough, and the Earth is changing enough, that I think God will soon be creating new forms of life.

"All the aquatic life can now be classed as either plant eaters or carnivorous. There are a few scavengers that will eat anything. Microscopic life too, is in a state of war. Sickness and disease testifies to the effectiveness of the control we have in all spheres."

Sure enough, abruptly, reports started coming in of amphibians of all sizes, shapes, and varieties. They were beautiful specimens and highly complex, created instantly and full grown.

The news spread so rapidly that it was assumed all had heard. Ah, but as usual, poor old Bucktooth had made himself scarce. His motto was, "What you don't understand, avoid." —and he didn't understand anything!

He hadn't even been able to make a microbe listen to him. Really, he hadn't even tried. It was just simply beyond his comprehension.

He shunned the lake like the plague, because of the fish. Now, he sleepily, strolled along the edge of a swampy marsh. As was his way, he was thinking of nothing at all.

He stepped between what he thought to be a log about ten

feet long and the marsh. It lay parallel to, and a couple feet from the muck of the swamp. He glanced at the log. It moved!

With a howl of terror, he landed waist deep in the soupy water. He paused for a moment, as he stared in horror at what he had taken to be a log.

As he watched, it raised a flat, bullet shaped head with small, black, beady eyes. It opened its mouth and a fiery red tongue about a foot long could be seen. With a banshee wail, Bucktooth went clear under. Realizing the danger of the swamp for the first time, he floundered back to the shore.

If he had looked at the large amphibian, which he was careful not to do, he would have seen that it was slowly crawling away from all this confusion. It didn't care for the situation any more than Bucktooth did!

At first, Bucktooth intended to run right to Lucifer. However, as his mind began to work, the idea didn't seem so good. Lucifer had a way of frightening him as much as the monster in the swamp.

His mind had enough to do with this latest problem that he didn't give his appearance any thought. Thus, Beelzebub broke into laughter when he came upon him. He was plastered with mud and seaweed. Some of it was wet and some beginning to dry. A long, slim leaf was still draped over one of his large, outstanding ears. He was sitting on a big flat stone, and trying, unsuccessfully, to think out his dilemma.

"Tain't funny, Beelzebub, I purt near got et by a munster what spits out fire!"

Bucktooth was obviously hurt that Beelzebub didn't take his experience seriously.

Sensing that a story was about to unfold, Beelzebub seated himself alongside Bucktooth, trying to be keep from getting muddy, himself.

Putting on a feigned sympathetic attitude, he asked, "That bad, huh? Tell me about it, Pal."

"Wal, ah was jist a walkin' 'long by the swamp, when a log turned into a whappin' dragon with glitterin' eyes full ah more evil than ya can imagine. He opened his mouth, an' pure fire spurted out. He'd a got me too, if'n ah hadn't jist got right down and outrun 'im!"

Beelzebub was all but strangling on his mirth, but didn't want to do anything that might stop the tale. At last, however, he could contain himself no longer. A chuckle got away from him as he tried to speak.

"Tell me, Bucktooth, did you run all the way on your hands and knees—right through the swamp? I don't see how you could have gotten so muddy any other way!"

Bucktooth looked pained, but was so engrossed in his story that he didn't let Beelzebub's light remark bother him too much.

"Oh, I was in the swamp, all right, ah jist ran right through it. It didn't even slow me up—much," he said, believing every word he said was true.

Beelzebub tired of the game quickly and explained, "That's all right, Bucktooth, this is just God's next step in creation. We're to get them started eating each other or at least fighting if they won't eat meat. If we can, we're to get them to eat fish and other water life as well."

"Ya jist go right ahead, Beelzebub. Them critters don't need a whole lot ah help ta git 'em ta eat things. Yah, and I fer one, have no intention ah bein' on their menu!"

After a few moments of silence, broken only by sounds of strangulation coming from Beelzebub, Bucktooth continued, "Ah still don't even have the ones ah cain't see under control. If'n ya don't mind, ah'll jist stick ta them fer a spell."

Now, Beelzebub was laughing out of control, and had gotten enough of Bucktooth's mud on his robe that he was going to have to do some laundry before he appeared in Lucifer's presence. The laugh was worth it, however.

Beelzebub arose with a final chuckle and slapped the troubled angel on the shoulder, raising a dust in the mud which had dried there. "Yah, Pal, I think that's a pretty good idea."

Relief visibly flowed through Bucktooth's whole frame. Now, for the first time, he began to think of his appearance. "My! How'd ah git so dirty? Ah don't even really remember bein' down in the mud. They's no two ways about it, though, ah'm goin' ta have ta go to the lake and wash mah robe and hair—possibly, even mah face! Uh shore hope they ain't no fishes about though!"

Orders for handling the amphibians were so similar to those for the fish and other water life that it had not been necessary to call a special meeting. Lucifer did warn his lieutenants, "Watch for new types of life, for I don't think it will be long before more creatures will appear. Be sure and warn your men."

Of course, the only one who hadn't been around to hear the warning was Bucktooth.

The swamp as well as the lake was now definitely off limits as far as he was concerned. He would not approach either except under threat of dire punishment. Bathing and laundry were done only in the presence of others and by direct orders.

Nodding vigorously to a grinning Beelzebub, and in the voice of an orator, Bucktooth said, "Beelzebub, ah done got it all figgered out. Water is safe only ta drink; but ya don't want ta drink too much. There might be some of them teeny little Miker—whatevers thet ya cain't even see in it!"

Hence, we find him sitting in the shade of a small tree in a pretty little upland park. The sun was warm and he was drowsy. He came wide awake when a beautiful butterfly lit on a stalk of a plant close by.

"How purty," he thought. "Kinda makes me think ah all the be-uty back in Heaven."

He decided to get a closer look, and of course, it fluttered away. While following it, he couldn't help thinking, "Boy, if all the life here were as purty as this'un, ah wouldn't be scairt ah none o' it, hardtly."

The thought had no more than struck him, when a tiny primitive mammal scurried past him to its den under a rock.

For a moment, Bucktooth's hair stood right on end. Seeing its diminutive size, he patted himself on the back for his bravery; and once more, set out to find his butterfly.

Across the glade, he saw the beautiful creature entering the forest. He didn't usually go in the forest; but after all, he had never seen anything up this high before except the little mammal—and certainly it wasn't dangerous. Anyway, wasn't he becoming pretty brave?

With a spring in his step, he took out after the insect so he wouldn't lose him in the trees. His prize always remained just far enough ahead of him that he couldn't quite get a good look at it. It led him into a thinly wooded canyon. He rounded a sharp bend, and wh-o-osh! The breath went out of him so completely that he couldn't even cry out.

Bucktooth had been given the dubious distinction of being the first one in Eden to discover a dinosaur!

For once in Bucktooth's life, he didn't run. He collapsed! For an interminable period of time, he lay watching the gigantic brute. Slowly, it ambled away. The farther it got, the more Bucktooth's courage returned; however, one could not normally accuse Bucktooth of foolhardiness. He was quite sure it was safe before making a move. In fact, the beast had rounded another bend in the canyon before Bucktooth deemed it wise to move at all.

Having survived the presence of the beast, and the first wave of terror, he decided that he would make an orderly and nonchalant entry. He would spread the news with dignity.

Starting back to camp, he did agree with himself that granting the aforementioned efforts at self-control, he hadn't ruled out haste between here and there.

He put thought to practice and legs to work. Thus, it was a short time, indeed, until he was back in the outer court.

"Lord Lucifer, Bucktooth is drawing a crowd again," commented Beelzebub.

"Hum, I wonder what he's found now. Bring him in," Lucifer ordered.

Bucktooth fairly strutted as he made his entry. Remembering his former encounters with new forms of life, Lucifer rather doubted his truthfulness. Knowing Bucktooth though, he did not want to frighten him in case he was telling the truth. In a kindly and comradely tone of voice, he asked, "Well, Bucktooth, what do you have for me this time?"

Bucktooth began importantly, "Wal Sir, ah was up in the high country inspectin' new kinds ah life—"

Lucifer interrupted him, "Kinds? How many did you find?"

"Yes Sir, kinds. Ah seen at least three."

"Start with the first one, and describe them all for me."

"All right, ta start with, there was this real purty kind of thing, almost as big as mah hand. It was mostly wings, which it flapped real slow. The colors of it was fancier than anythin' ah've seen since ah left Heaven."

The high-ranking angels standing around the throne were nodding their heads. This was not the first time these had been described.

"And the next one?"

"Wal sir, this'n ah didn't git too good a look at; but it was brown and furry. Oh yes, an' it had teeth somethin' like mine."

Again, there were the nods, this time accompanied with smiles.

Lucifer was slowly becoming impressed. Maybe this goof would be good for something after all.

"All right, my friend, now the last one," and he smiled encouragingly to keep the tall goof talking freely.

Lucifer was even more convinced when he noticed the shudder that ran over Bucktooth. He had at least seen something!

Bucktooth hesitated, seemingly at loss for words to describe the last one. Again he started out with his familiar, "Wal Sir," and continued, "it was so big that big don't even tell it. I suppose it was as high as this room."

Eyebrows raised at this, but after the accurate descriptions he had been giving, no one interrupted him.

"His legs were almost as big around as your throne, and he was almost as long as this hall."

Watching Bucktooth's features, it was obvious that the mere recollection terrified him. No one believed that the creature was as big as he said. None doubted, however, that he had seen it, and believed it as he told it.

"What did it look like?" asked a natty, duded up angel with cute little ruffles on strategic parts of his robe.

"It was a heavy built critter, Dandy," observed Bucktooth. "And it had a large fringe of bone that stuck back from its head and covered its shoulders. It had a wallopin' hooked beak, sorta like Eagle back in Heaven has." He paused for a moment to think. "Yah, and it had three great horns stickin' out'ah it's head."

No doubt about now, there were dinosaurs in Eden! Lucifer nodded to Apollyon, who spun on his heel to go see just what these creatures were.

With the advent of the dinosaurs, Apollyon came into his own. There were many types that he enjoyed working with. His favorite, however, was a tall, swift fellow with strong hind legs. It had little almost useless front ones, and a mighty mow of a mouth full of teeth. He had the mind, intelligence, and disposition of a crocodile! Thousands of years later, man would name him from his bones. His name would be, Tyrannosaurus Rex, The tyrant King!

It would be no accident that the mighty beast would be so named; for Apollyon the Destroyer would be riding upon his shoulder, so to speak.

Apollyon took off to see first hand how things were going, worldwide. In spite of their efforts, it seemed there was always a group of creatures in all types who simply refused to eat meat. Most of them would fight over food, a mate, or other selfish motives, though. All hands had to be reminded never to let up on selfishness as a means of attack.

As Apollyon levitated along, he spotted a large bunch of animals below. All of them seemed to be getting along disgustingly well. Approaching, he saw for the first time, the great Tyrannosaurus mingling peaceably with the rest of the animals.

Of all the creatures represented in the clearing, the huge dinosaur was all he had eyes for. Here was his dinosaur! Never again would any animal dine peaceably with this fellow!

Old Mrs. Primitive Mammal munched contentedly. She scurried right along side the great giant. Never having had to fear him, she gave him no thought. Her seven tiny babies were at home under the old hollow tree, and would be hungry pretty soon. She planned to finish the delectable green plant she was eating, and then go feed them.

The approach of Apollyon, of course, was undetected by any except Tyrannosaurus. A strange stirring took place within his mind. For the first time in his life, he had a craving for flesh.

Snap! It happened so quickly that the rest of the animals didn't even realize a tragedy had taken place. No more would Mrs. Mammal browse upon tender green plants. Her babies would soon awake and squeak pitifully. Never again would Momma come to them. They would cry their baby lives away. Sin had entered their realm!

Mighty Tyrannosaurus's teeth would adapt to flesh, and he would dine on nothing else.

Apollyon was delighted. If the ease with which he had been able to take over the mighty animal's mind was any example, he would have a blast with him.

Grazing a short distance away was a gigantic herbivore. It was six or seven times the size of Rex. Here would be a good test for his new plaything.

This beast possessed no diplomacy. His roar scattered the smaller animals in the clearing, sending them scurrying for cover as they would always do from now on at the approach of Tyrannosaurus Rex. Ferociously, he attacked the great neighbor, who was guilty only of minding his own business.

"You may refuse to eat meat, you stupid hulk," thought Apollyon, "but I'll bet you'll fight when your skin is at stake!"

For a moment, it seemed he wouldn't. Fighting was just too foreign to his nature. Apollyon thought, "Oh, for the love of Mike. It isn't even going to be interesting at this rate!"

Switching his attention from Rex, Apollyon concentrated upon the large herbivore for a while. Rex was doing so well that he really didn't need to keep his mind on him.

Rex had the beast by his long neck, and was not long from dining upon dinosaur steak when Apollyon got through to

Rex's victim. The huge creature shook himself much as a dog would upon coming out of the water.

Rex staggered back, momentarily having lost his balance. It would be a few more moments before he regained it. A forty-foot tail lashed like a whip, catching him about shoulder high. Rex turned end over end. He resembled a giant football bouncing into the end zone. For a few moments, he thought maybe the game should be called off.

Such was not to be the case; however, for Apollyon had inserted another element into the mind of the naturally peaceful herbivore: rage!

Apollyon was not capable of true loyalty. His likes were totally selfish. In spite of how well he liked Rex, if the herbivore could kill him, so what? Tough-o! That's the way the ball bounces. He'd just find himself another dinosaur.

As the big dinosaur bore in on Rex, there was nothing but murder in his heart. Rex rolled aside, forgetting his bruises. The blood lust returned as Apollyon switched his attention to him, and the fight was on.

It had been a beautiful, peaceful glade, inhabited by a lovely assortment of God's creatures. Now it became a torn battleground occupied by two murderous giants bent upon killing and vengeance.

Herbivore was obviously getting the worst of the exchange. He was bleeding from huge gashes all over his body. It would only be a matter of time until he died by bleeding to death. The blood lust was still running high in Rex, and he lacked anything resembling patience. Never would he settle for waiting for a victim to bleed to death. He would attack until all motion and resistance ceased.

Herbivore was tiring and ceased his struggles for a few moments. Rex stood erect to look around, thinking his victim dead. While Rex was standing thus, Herbivore gave one last desperate lash of his mighty tail. The blow was not nearly as hard as the earlier one, but he caught Rex across his soft unprotected stomach. Rex went rolling as much in pain as by the force of the blow. He retaliated instantly, ripping the throat from the great beast, and ending his suffering.

Rex's suffering was just beginning; however, for that last blow had done irreparable damage to him internally. He would wander away in pain, never eating a bite of the meal he had fought so hard to attain.

Apollyon continued on, pleased as a child with a new toy. There would, doubtlessly, be many more of the Tyrannosaurus Rexes. That had truly, been a fight worth watching. He would have to keep his eye out for more of these creatures!

He would also have to explain more fully to his subordinates, the importance of instilling the instinct of self-preservation. That would be under the heading of selfishness. In fact, it probably should head the list. Blood lust was also very important, as he had seen today. Pure rage could be used quite handily when all else failed, and a thirst for vengeance would keep a fight going when hunger and all else had been forgotten.

Hunger should not be sold short, though. After acquiring a taste for flesh,[10] this would be a formidable drive.

CHAPTER VII

PRIMATES

It started out as simply a routine report. The messenger finally described a creature that walked upright, though somewhat bent over. It rested its knuckles on the ground as it traveled. It stood between a foot and a half and two feet high. It had hands and arms similar to the angels only longer accordingly.

Lucifer had been relaxed and leaning back in his seat. Now he sat on the leading edge of the chair, leaning forward as he spoke.

"You idiot!" He spat his words out like bullets. His vicious stare pierced the unhappy wretch like a knife. "This is the news I've been waiting for every since we came here, and you waste an hour on nonsense before telling me about it!"

"I-I'm sorry, my Lord," he stammered. "I didn't realize how important it was."

Lucifer's eyes snapped, "You didn't realize, period. Now get me one. I want it here where I can examine it."

"But—but how am I to get it to come?" stuttered the hapless individual.

"Kill it, if you have to!" roared Lucifer.

After the messenger left, Lucifer confided to Dandy, "I am sure this can't be 'Man', but I can't take any chances."

After a lengthy pause, he continued, "I believe I'll send out an all points alert. If there is one of them, there will be many.

God seems to be creating entire populations of each kind of animal when He creates any of them."

For the first time since Lucifer came to Earth, he was definitely restless. He could not sit still, and paced the length of the inner sanctum. The messenger hadn't been gone over a couple hours, and the universal capture order globe wide less than an hour when he began to fret at the delay.

"You would think, with the whole world out to get one, that it wouldn't take forever to deliver it, wouldn't you?"

All who were there hastened to agree with him. Those who had business to attend to got it done and exited quickly. Those who were stationed there could only count the minutes until they were relieved.

Two days elapsed before one was finally bagged. They were extremely intelligent, quick, and agile. They also appeared to be rather immune to Lucifer's mind control techniques for the time being. One could not help wondering if the Lord wasn't having a little fun at Lucifer's expense. One could also imagine two great angels and the beasts by the screen, rooting for the tiny primate.

Alas, though, Lucifer ruled upon Earth. It was a foregone conclusion that he would win in the end.

Ramapithecus—for such would be his name in years to come when men found his bones—would be caught.

If Lucifer's followers thought the heat would let up after the successful capture of the little upright monkey, they were sadly mistaken! For one thing, he showed too much intelligence. Lucifer felt threatened even before it had been caught. Its display of brilliance sealed its doom before he had ever seen it.

Pandemonium in the outer court heralded the approach of the successful capture party. Three angels burst into the inner sanctum with a squeaking, kicking, biting, scratching little monkey. The leader of the party handed it to Lucifer with its mouth still fastened securely to his thumb.

Lucifer made no attempt to take it. Disdainfully, he ordered, "Set it down." In a display of mind control intended to demonstrate his superiority, and make all envious; he concentrated upon the little fellow, who sat down quietly while Lucifer examined him.

Several hours later, Lucifer said, "The intelligence tests show that he's an intelligent little animal, but he's no threat to such a being as an angel."

Racking his memory, Lucifer was sure that he could remember several primates before man when he had seen the preview in Heaven. His mind had been in such turmoil; however, that it had sort of gone blank. Almost, it seemed that the memories of the primates had been erased from his mind. To start with, the primates were just animals. He just simply hadn't paid enough attention.

Oh! If he had only had presence of mind enough to realize that he would rebel and need this knowledge later on! It would have eliminated so much worry now!

Never would he have admitted any lack of perfection to anyone else. Secretly, he was certainly kicking himself for this lack now.

In exasperation, he swung a savage karate chop; and the little primate lay kicking at his feet.

"Feed him to the crocodiles," he ordered, "then spread the word. I want this species entirely eliminated! Hinder them in every way possible. They are not the species I was thinking about, but these will be good practice for when they do arrive. These are stupid compared to that one."

Again, messengers blanketed the Earth, "Rampithecus must die!" This was the first specific order of its kind—the extermination of a species! Other species would have inadvertently become extinct due to the harassment of the fallen angels, but this was extinction by executive order!

Where were they to be found? At this point, all the sightings had been in the jungles and forested areas.

The fallen angels in the plains and tundras rejoiced. The ones in the jungles mopped their brows and got ready for a long fight. If Lucifer got impatient, as they were sure he would, life wasn't going to be much fun for any of his followers.

Every predator in the jungle and forest abruptly developed a taste for monkey. A drink of water became a treat acquired at the peril of one's life. Huge crocodiles lurked in the larger bodies of water. Alligators lay in wait in the streams. Water snakes competed with the 'gators and crocs, while their tree climbing cousins hunted for them before they even got to the water.

The ground was a no man's land of reptilian predators. Their minds were under the control of the fallen angels, and suddenly they really liked monkey meat.

Also, large wolflike creodants were running in packs on every hand. Saber-toothed cats also entered the fray. Early primitive birds tried to snatch them out of the trees. Still, the little monkey with the great big name would not be eliminated!

The monkey was losing the battle in the jungle. Being a creature of no mean intelligence, the smarter individuals started creeping out onto the plains. As of yet, the attack was not so centralized and intense there.

The tall grass was at the same time, a blessing and a curse. The small primates were harder to see. As long as they remained constantly alert, they fared quite well. However, any lapse of concentration might place them on top of a predator who was taking the same advantage of the cover.

Food now became a serious problem. The jungle had supplied such an abundance of vegetation, that our little friend had resisted all attempts to cause him to eat flesh. Now though, in his harried existence, food became food. It didn't make any difference whether it was a fat snail, worm, or grub. If it supplemented his meager vegetative menu, it was welcome.

His legs grew stronger as he became used to running. Now, he learned another vital truth: Even a tiny monkey is formidable in combat if there are enough monkeys!

Little Rampithecus could have taken a certain amount of consolation, had he known it, from the fact that he had made life on Earth a living Hell for the forces of evil that were at work to destroy him. Lucifer was livid with rage when his men couldn't even wipe out one little monkey in a reasonably short time.

Those who had sold out to Lucifer for power and position would gladly have traded places with those at the bottom of the command chain. Facing Lucifer with a negative report was not a picnic by any stretch of the imagination! After stepping up once, admitting failure, and suffering the consequences, you tried not to do that again. What followed was enough to cause them to wring every bit of effort out of themselves and their followers in the future! Yes, and failure seemed to be the name of the game with the little monkey!

The little fellow's battle for survival was heroic. For a while, it even looked as though he might survive in spite of the odds. But the hordes of Hell were solidly against him. It was a foregone conclusion that sooner or later, the last little monkey would find himself in the jaws of some predator, which was driven on by some evil angel.

"Apollyon! Beelzebub! Rege! We need to throw a party to reward the troops for destroying this pesky little monkey!" said the now beaming Lucifer.

"Wonderful work men! We'll win this war yet!" chortled Lucifer. "Help yourself! There are drugs, alcohol, anything and everything—a kick for every taste!"

"There will be some broken heads and headaches in the morning," Beelzebub said with a grin.

"Serves them right," Apollyon returned with a sneer.

In the great throne room in Heaven, the mood was anything but festive. Gabriel sat in brooding silence. Michael paced to let off pent up emotion. A pall of sorrow seemed to surround all. These were emotions which seemed to be so out of place where joy had always reigned.

The silence was finally broken by Michael, "Great, powerful, mighty Lucifer!" With his words fairly dripping sarcasm, he continued, "Strut, Lucifer, Star of the Morning. Haven't you just destroyed one cute, innocent little monkey from the face of the Earth? Man! You're the greatest!"

"Easy, My warrior chieftain," the Lord said, soothingly. "I too, think that if they suppose they are so wonderful after destroying our little primate, that they should have something to really test their skill. It is also a shame for such an evil party to have anything but an unhappy ending."

Squad 666, Beelzebub's old bunch of ne'r-do-wells and losers, were having a party of their own. Why go to Eden and risk being chewed out if you can avoid it?

The party had lasted all night. As dawn began to lighten up the jungle, one bleary-eyed individual stepped out of their tent for a breath of fresh air. He stretched and strolled out into the center of the clearing.

In Heaven, the crystal screen zoomed in on this particular clearing. From experience, everyone knew that something interesting was about to take place. They watched with bated breath. The Angel of the Lord raised His hand, and the order to create went out.

Immediately, the entire Earth was populated with a new species of primate. Today, men see the same type of animal in the gorilla cage at the zoo. The nearest thing to his size, however, would be the movie industry's King Kong. Yes, and everybody knew you didn't give no lip to—Gigantopithecus!

Our bleary-eyed member of Squad 666 never had any idea how it happened. All he knew was that he found himself face to face with a huge bull gorilla. The giant ape was taller than he was, even though it was on all fours. Its ham like hands were planted solidly on the ground, resting on their knuckles.

The bleary eyes cleared and became saucer round in an instant. In mid stride, he spun and dashed for the tent. When he got about six feet from the tent, he simply plunged in. He came head first, sliding through the flaps on his stomach. He slid up against the back of the tent and rolled over. Unable to speak, he simply pointed a trembling finger in the direction from which he had come.

Nervous's head snapped around to look out of the flaps, and then his mouth began to work without sound. Finally, he stuttered, "L-l-look!"

Everyone crowded to the door for a look to see what had frightened their pals so much.

With his audience assembled, the gigantic gorilla stood

erect and beat his mighty chest. His roar seemed to fairly shake the Earth. What else he did, Squad 666 couldn't have told you. They hadn't hung around to watch!

In fact, his roar hadn't died in his throat when the whole squad, led by Bleary Eyes and Nervous, emerged from the back of the tent. There hadn't been a door there, but that wouldn't make any difference anymore. Now there wasn't even a back in the tent.

The two mighty creatures back in Heaven simply collapsed into a mound of merriment. Tears of mirth gushed from their eyes as they laughed until they simply ran out of breath. Gabriel lay back against the throne, holding his sides. Michael, though enjoying the scene, was more under control. Even while laughing, he couldn't help wondering what Lucifer's next move would be.

The party in Eden was still going full blast when Squad 666 crashed the gate. They had apparently been the first to discover the huge ape. Their news acted like a bucket of water on the celebrants. These now, suddenly become cold sober. As bad as it had been with the little monkey, what was war with this monster going to be?

Lucifer's eyes were squinted, and his mouth formed a white bloodless line on his face. Motioning to his lieutenants, he ordered, "Bring them into the inner sanctum."

Abruptly, Squad 666 wished they were back in their tent—or even facing Gigantopithecus in their clearing.

"What do they look like?" Lucifer demanded.

Bleary Eyes shrugged, held his arm straight up with his wrist bent and his hand parallel to the ground. "They're about this high, when they're on all fours. They're real heavy built. They ain't got a tail like a monkey."

"No tail?" Lucifer repeated as though it were an accusation.

"No Sir."

Lucifer looked the squad over with a gaze which made each cringe as it went past, and thought, "I'm not going to get much more of use out of these losers. I'll just have to send out someone who at least has enough brains to tell me what I need to know."

Abruptly, he seemed to take a new thought trend.

"Who is taking care of your district while all of you are gone?

They looked at each other in surprise. Until right now, they hadn't even thought that they had deserted their post.

"But—but that monster ape is there!"

Lucifer sneered sarcastically, "What a shame! You worthless fool! You are going to control their minds, and help destroy them just as we did the monkey! Just because they're big doesn't make their minds any harder to control than if they were little. If you bums had been doing your jobs correctly, you wouldn't have thought anything about being afraid of them!"

Suddenly, the mighty apes didn't seem nearly as dangerous as Lucifer. When he turned his back on them, Weasel Face squeaked, "I think it's about time for us to go home!"

Droopy Drawers looked fearfully at Lucifer's back, and said in a stage whisper, "Yah, if he's through with us, before he decides to put us somewheres else. —or even worse, keeps us here."

Lucifer walked out where he could look around at his party goers. "You guys go ahead and have fun. I've got things I need to do."

Lucifer left and so did squad 666.

The smiling Lucifer was gone. Now the look on his face didn't make anyone feel at ease.

Lucifer paced, screamed, and roared. Again, the inner sanctum had become a no man's land to be avoided at all costs if possible. One simply endured it when one had to be in there. Anyone within the confines of Eden was much too easily found and ordered into the inner sanctum. Even receiving simple orders from Lucifer was an ordeal to leave one trembling and shaken by the time they could escape.

"Squad leaders and other angels of rank are to remain until a decision can be made as to what to do about this newest creation," Lucifer ordered.

"I really think these have to be too big to be man, but man won't have a tail. We really have to look them over carefully. Use as much of the knowledge that you gleaned from the monkey as is pertinent. —but destroy them all!

"Due to their size, you can cause them to be ill-tempered. Get them to fighting among themselves and other large, dangerous animals. Maybe they'll cause their own extinction," Lucifer ordered.

In this last respect, to an extent at least, they had outsmarted themselves. In a very short time, all the great carnivores had learned that to attack, or even stand their ground against a family group of giant gorillas was a good way to attain one's own extinction!

Beelzebub, in a way, was receiving a good many of his just desserts. Because of his position, he was always in reach of Lucifer's acid tongue. Even though they both needed the other, they found one another a burden very hard to bear.

Beelzebub, at times, even envied Bucktooth. Due to his low mentality, nothing seemed to be demanded of him. Beelzebub would have hated to be in Bucktooth's shoes forever, but there were times that a week or two would sure have felt good.

Beelzebub reflected back on his old Squad 666 when they brought in the gorilla report. He couldn't help thinking that Bucktooth could almost do as well as they had. At least, he couldn't fail a whole lot more. While on this thought trend, he had a brain wave that was brilliant if he did say so himself.

Even with his good idea, he hated to enter the inner sanctum. If he were to get away from Lucifer for a little while, however, he would have to see him first. Yes, and the sooner he got that nasty job over the better.

As he walked through the outer court, few even looked up, let alone showed him the respect that one of his rank should have.

"No wonder," he thought, "the way Lucifer treats me, no one is going to respect me. Then he expects nothing but perfection of me when I have an assignment."

Beelzebub was having himself quite a pity party. If things went right, though, he would make up for some of these injustices while away from Eden.

Lucifer was speaking to an angel of lesser rank when Beelzebub came slinking up. Lucifer continued to talk to the first angel, even though Beelzebub could tell that the conversation was really not that important.

"Typical," thought Beelzebub.

At last, Lucifer pierced Beelzebub with his deadly black eyes and growled, "What do you want?"

Beelzebub almost lost his nerve. Since he was already there, and he didn't have a lot to lose, he got himself together and began, "Master, I've just had a great idea!"

"About time someone did!"

"Yes Sir, it sure is," said Beelzebub ingratiatingly, and continued, "I've been thinking about groups such as that Squad 666 that came in here yesterday, and others like them. It is possible that they might shape up if we were to spring a few surprise inspections on them. And, I would like permission to take charge of the inspections."

Lucifer took a very long time to think it over. The idea was, indeed, good; but he couldn't let Beelzebub think that he had thought up anything so good as to gain instant acceptance. The best part of the idea was that he wouldn't have to have this necessary, but creepy little turkey around for a while.

Slowly, almost grudgingly, he agreed. "All right, and while you are there, see to it that Squad 666 knows how to handle those oversized monkeys." Almost as an afterthought, he continued, "And take Bucktooth with you. I don't think it's possible, but he might learn something."

"Thank you, oh thanks, Master!"

Lucifer snarled, "Oh, get out of here!"

Now he had to find Bucktooth. He really didn't mind taking the skinny goof. He was good for a laugh or two along. Also, he had a way of making Beelzebub feel like he was somebody after all.

The only problem was to find him. If there was anything Bucktooth was expert at, it was making himself scarce.

Almost, it seemed he had an animal like ability to blend and disappear where there wasn't anything to blend into of disappear behind. There seemed to be nothing Lucifer wished for him to do that he could do, or wanted to do.

Beelzebub did have one advantage in finding him. For some reason, Bucktooth liked him and didn't fear him. Even so, a good portion of the District of Eden had been covered before Beelzebub finally located him—perhaps we should say, Bucktooth found Beelzebub.

As Beelzebub walked along, Bucktooth stepped out from behind a bush and was walking beside him. He did it so smoothly that he was shoulder to shoulder with him before Beelzebub even knew he was there.

Beelzebub jumped and then scolded, "Bucktooth!

Where in the world have you been? I've looked everywhere for you!"

Bucktooth looked hurt, and Beelzebub slapped him on the shoulder in a comradely manner to show that there were no hard feelings. He wanted Bucktooth to wish to come with him, and couldn't afford to offend him. As a last resort, he could tell him that Lucifer had ordered him to go; but he knew that if it came to that, the trip wouldn't be nearly so pleasant.

Continuing the comradely air, he gurgled, "You would never guess what I get to do, not in a million years!"

Beelzebub had guaged his man well. Bucktooth reacted as a small child would.

"Aw, come on, Beelzebub, tell me. Ah won't tell if'in ya don't want me to—please!"

"It is kind of a secret," Beelzebub said, "for we don't want the outlying squads to know I'm going to do it—but if you promise—"

"Oh! Ah promise!" cried Bucktooth, almost beside himself.

"All right, I'm going to be going all over the world making

surprise inspections of the different groups of angels. We need to make sure they are doing their work."

Bucktooth's enthusiasm died as though it had been doused in cold water. His head dropped, and he shuffled his feet. Finally looking up, he stuttered, "Ya—ya mean ah'm goin' ta be left here all alone?"

Beelzebub heaved a sigh of relief, but he could not resist twisting the knife a little. "You won't be alone, Bucktooth. There'll be all kinds of folks around."

"Yah, but ut won't be the same with y'all gone."

Beelzebub took on an air of conspiracy, and whispered behind his hand, "If I could talk Lucifer into it, would you like to go along?"

Bucktooth cried, "Oh, Beelzebub! You know I would." Visible relief simply flowed through him.

"Now wait a minute. I haven't talked to Lucifer," lied Beelzebub, "and if he agrees, I'm not going to comb Eden looking for you. You hang around where I can find you. All right? Otherwise, I'll leave without you. Understand?"

"You bet!" Bucktooth never doubted that Beelzebub could pull it off. Of course, he never thought to wonder why Beelzebub should have been walking around out in the wilds that far from camp looking for him either.

This really worked out nicely. Bucktooth would be coming willingly. While Beelzebub was supposed to be talking to Lucifer, in reality, he would be finishing up some last minute details he had to see to. Best of all, he'd be able to find Bucktooth!

Daybreak found Beelzebub and Bucktooth levitating away from Eden. Both—though for different reasons—were very happy to be gone.

Beelzebub decided to leave the squads close to Eden to the last. Because of their being so readily available to the District of Eden, they tended to be more on the ball anyway. No, he would get as far away as possible before making a move. Then, he should really be able to shock some folks before the news got around that he was inspecting them.

His move was a huge success. Many modern military men may recognize his influence in past and present drill sergeants! Life had been pretty easy for these out of the way squads, and none were really ready for Beelzebub.

Appearing right in their midst, he would shout, "At'shun! Front and center—form up!"

Since his own clothes were clean, but nothing to brag about otherwise, he didn't upbraid them about the condition of theirs, just their cleanness. Raving like a mad man, he would exclaim, "Where is your loyalty, or integrity? You are in one of the best places on Earth. Don't you even have simple appreciation enough to do a decent days work?"

After pacing and raving, he would just pace and glare for a while before beginning over again.

Bucktooth thought, "Loyalty? Integrity? Appreciation? I hain't seed any ah that since ah been down here!"

Bucktooth was beginning to learn a little. This enabled him to ask, "Beelzebub, why is it that everythin' we is supposed ta do brings only pain and heartache? Ah hain't seed anythin' done yet what was good."

Beelzebub stared at the tall goof in slack-jawed amazement. He reflected a moment after regaining his composure. Finally, he decided he didn't have the ability to get through to Bucktooth about the fine points of the situation, and settled with a stern warning.

"Bucktooth, don't ever let anyone else hear you say anything like that. If Lucifer even knew you had thought such a thing, goodness knows what he would do to you." Even Beelzebub shuddered and proceeded, "I know you can do a good job of hiding, but the world isn't big enough for you to hide in if he really put out a contract on you!"

Bucktooth was very contrite and humble in his reply, "Ah'm shore sorry, Beelzebub. Ah didn't mean ta say anythin' wrong. An ah'll shore be careful from now on!"

Bucktooth would be as good as his word, too. He had become quite a loner anyway. Now, knowing that he could get himself in trouble by saying the wrong thing, and not really knowing what was wrong with what he had said, silence would, indeed, be golden.

Both had been traveling along in silence. Looking below, Beelzebub found himself above the clearing that was home to Squad 666—his old pals.

With a look of vicious glee, Beelzebub prepared to make his entrance. The back of the tent had been repaired in a fashion typical of the squad. Long looping stitches had been taken. Air and light made easy entrance between each one. The entire crew was seated around a crude table. It looked as though they were playing some sort of game that resembled modern cards. The only thing they were doing a good job of was shouting and cursing at each other for real or imagined injustices.

They all were still rather jittery from their brush with Gigantopithecus. Baggy Eyes, who was seated with his back to the rear of the tent, looked up and saw Beelzebub standing in the tent flap. The shock he registered was enough to cause all to land on their feet in a shower of table, chairs, and cards.

The fact that these guys were his old friends from back in Heaven didn't hinder Beelzebub a bit. "Very good," he crooned. He was, himself, amused enough to be having a little trouble keeping from showing his mirth. However, he soon warmed to his sadistic work.

Beelzebub pulled a white glove from within his robe and ran it under the table. It came out covered with not only dust, but food, mold, and several compounds which he had never before come in contact with. He glared around the tent, and began to chant: "Rotten food, dirty dishes, foul clothes—do you ever do dishes or laundry? He glanced down at himself. Since he was in Eden most of the time, his clothes were quite a bit cleaner than theirs, if every bit as shabby. "—and just who is handling the wild life in your district while you are all in here playing?"

Sheepishly, Droopy Drawers admitted, "No one, I guess."

With this, Beelzebub began all over again. "Look, you bums, there are many very nice districts bordering Eden. We just might put you there where we can fellowship like in the good old days!" The sarcasm in his voice and the glint in his eye sent chills up their spines. "—and if you don't shape up, that is where you will be stationed!"

Their faces showed that this obviously didn't appeal to anyone, but none dared to voice any objection.

"Beelzebub, do you ever miss just being one of the guys?" asked Droopy Drawers.

Beelzebub thought back to his experiences just before he left Eden, and thought, "Yah, I do."

As though he were awakening from a dream, Beelzebub snapped, "Shut up! Just shut up, Droopy!"

Then, in mock solemnity, Beelzebub said, "All right, children, we are going on a field trip. I am under orders to teach you how to handle these big monkeys you are so afraid of; and there is no time like the present!"

Beelzebub strutted off like a little turkey gobbler, followed by a very sullen Squad 666. They were not long in finding their quarry. In obvious good humor, two great bulls and a female were in a clearing, working the fruit trees around the edge. Beelzebub instructed the squad, "Listen, jerks, blend your minds with mine so you can learn to control them as I do."

Beelzebub concentrated on the two mighty males, and they soon were showing signs of hostility. Abruptly, one leaped upon the other, and the fight was on. Biting, kicking, and punching, they rolled over and over in the tall grass. They then broke apart, and ran whooping and roaring around the park, throwing rocks and sticks.

Weasel Face nudged Droopy Drawers, and soon all were in whispered conversation. With Beelzebub distracted, they too were in deep concentration on the female. She stirred and began to look around.

Beelzebub was in such deep concentration that he didn't see her coming until she was within reach. With a happy gurgle from way down in her barrel chest, large hairy arms clasped the kicking, struggling Beelzebub to her ample bosom.

Beelzebub fought, shrieked, and blubbered as she showered him with slobbering kisses with her great, flaplike lips.

In Beelzebub's panic, he didn't think to use his supernatural ability to disappear. It had never been necessary before, and even angels are creatures of habit.

The giant female was doing so well now that Squad 666 switched their attention to the two mighty males. Seeing the female making such ardent love to Beelzebub, they forgot their own quarrel as jealousy gripped their hearts.

In a combined, roaring charge, both attacked at once. A tug-of-war ensued with Beelzebub acting as the unwilling rope. It was hard to tell which was the hardest on him, his loving captor or the hate filled antagonists.

Beelzebub's panic subsided, and his presence of mind returned. With the return of thought, he simply vanished as he became intangible.

The huge gorillas milled around in bewilderment for some time. They then ambled off, not quite able to remember what all the confusion had been about.

When the apes finally worked their way out of sight, the entire horde of fallen angels, again, took on tangible form. A bruised and livid Beelzebub stamped his feet, waved his arms, and stuck his finger right under their noses. He raved, "You creeps really want to work right there in Eden, don't you? I'll see you there where Lucifer can wipe his feet on you every day! Your life of leisure is over! Don't think he can't reduce you to one part beings! He can kill you, and you'll go through eternity as formless spirits!"

Beelzebub ran out of breath and verbal inspiration suddenly. He, without another word, just turned and left.

No doubt about it, this could be a serious situation. Even so, Squad 666 had to snicker every time they thought of Beelzebub in the clutches of the lovelorn female ape.

Bucktooth had at first been worried about his pal, and couldn't see the funny side of it. After he saw all was well; however, he too, had quite a problem keeping a straight face. Knowing Beelzebub as he did; though, he knew that this definitely was no time for laughter!

Gone was any joy that Beelzebub might have been having in his new job. Vengeance was all he could think about. In his fury, he charted a course straight for Eden.

Beelzebub burst into the inner sanctum, and never even noticed that he was receiving the respect he had longed for earlier. His wrath was etched into every line of his face, from the snarl on his lips to the squint of his eyes. There wasn't an angel in the building who didn't stand back to give him room.

In choking spasms, he told of his experience, "It was awful, Master! She slobbered all over my face. She handled my whole body, and then when the males showed up, she nearly tore me in two!"

As Beelzebub proceeded, Lucifer snickered in spite of himself. The snicker turned to a chuckle; which even caused his stomach to jiggle. Finally, his laughter poured from his wide-open mouth like water from a broken cup.

Beelzebub's expression turned to shock as Lucifer slid down in his seat till he was nearly prone. Beelzebub simply wilted. No one had ever seen Lucifer laugh like this before. They hadn't thought it was in him.

This was icing on the cake for those watching in Heaven. Lovable and Sweet Thing fairly split while watching the she ape making love to Beelzebub. Everything he got, he so richly deserved; now this, and the end was not in sight.

When Lucifer got his breath back and became serious, he observed with something of a chuckle in his voice, "It does appear that they have mastered the use of mind control, doesn't it, Beelzebub?"

Beelzebub responded just enough to stay out of trouble.

Lucifer then continued, "I don't believe you are quite cut out for this kind of work, my friend. I believe we will have Apollyon take over from now on. When he's to busy, he can send Rege. Dismissed."

Beelzebub slumped out of the room, lost in thought. "A fine thing this is. This is the reward I get for following Lucifer. The price of sin is, indeed, high. I work hard, take all kinds of guff, get insulted, and beat up. What does Lucifer do? He just laughs at me, insults me, and fires me in spite of the fact that I did what he sent me out to do. Worse yet, then he just simply dismisses me."

As he walked out the door, he thought, "Yes, Droopy, there are times I miss being just one of the guys!"

Bucktooth hadn't exited for the rough country yet when Beelzebub came out. Seeing his friend so sad, he threw a comforting arm around his shoulders.

"What's the matter with ya, Beelzebub?"

"Oh, Lucifer just laughed at me and gave my job to Apollyon." Beelzebub's head hung until his chin touched his chest, and he couldn't even meet Bucktooth's eyes.

"Aw, that's to bad. I'm really sorry fer ya."

Looking up at his gawky friend, Beelzebub mused, "You know, Bucktooth, you're the only good thing I've seen on this planet. I'm not just sure what the future has in store for you. You just don't seem to fit."

Bucktooth didn't really understand what Beelzebub was talking about. He replied, "Shucks, Beelzebub, as long as ah have a friend like you, ah'll do all right."

Beelzebub thought, "Little does he know that I wouldn't let him stand in my way to the top for a moment. As long as it's convenient, I'll use him. After that, he's on his own."

Things were happening more and more rapidly on Earth, and Beelzebub didn't have long to brood. Reports started coming in of a smaller type of gorilla.

Lucifer went 'Ape' himself. Eden was becoming more of a Hell all the time.

Right on the heels of the ape report, chimpanzees and monkeys whole sale were sighted. For the fallen angels, Earth as well as Eden was becoming more hellish.

Almost, it seemed that God was flooding the Earth with primates to such an extent that it would be impossible for Lucifer and his crew to ever catch up.

As unreasoning as Lucifer's rage was, slowly, it was becoming plain to him that he was not going to win this round. Up to this point, virtually everything he had wanted to do or have on Earth, he had done or had.

Finally, in the bitterness of his soul, he sent out the order, "Ease up on the smaller primates, and concentrate on Gigantopithecus. Hinder the smaller ones when it is handy."

CHAPTER VIII

PREADAMIC MAN

The giant ape was not to give up easily. It would take twice as long to bring him to extinction as it did little Ramapithecus. The fact was, he was quite able to take care of himself in most any kind of disagreement!

Two exquisite upright apes would appear in the last half of his history on Earth. They would buy him some time, Lucifer some gray hair, and the fallen angels a haggard, whipped, hangdog look.

Turning to Dandy, who was holding a mirror at arms length to see his wavy hair and pencil line mustache, Lucifer said, "You know, Dandy, I think it is time for a first. I think I better go out and examine these last ones for myself. They sound a little too human to me."

It was an elaborate, gold trimmed sedan chair, carried by muscular, bare-chested angels. The procession was preceded by large, blond, carbon-copies of the bearers. They were blowing long golden horns as they entered the area where many of the two types that seemed prevalent were to be found.

An impatient Lucifer frowned from within. Wouldn't you believe that they were more than usually shy today? Bloody Red, the leader of the troop, mopped his brow and reflected, under his breath, "There really doesn't seem to be any rest for the wicked—squad leaders in particular! At last, a specimen was found, and Lucifer put his mind-bending power to work. The creature obviously wanted to flee, but a power greater than its own was demanding that it not only stop, but return. These creatures were of a high enough order that they did have a certain power to resist. The mental struggle going on in its ape like head was discernible to all. Alas, it was still an animal, and in Lucifer's realm. It would return to its fate.

Lucifer examined it with care. It was a young female, possibly pregnant, and probably would have been considered attractive by those of her own species.

Lucifer reflected at length before coming to a conclusion. "Really, I'm quite sure she is subhuman; however, she is much too humanoid to be ruled out. Her entire species must be destroyed. They will be given top priority!"

So saying, he aimed a deft blow that left her struggling at his feet with a broken neck.

On the way back to Eden, Lucifer was almost pleasant. True, the troublesome new species would have to be dealt with, but at least he had been able to do something concrete, himself, today. Hadn't he eliminated two of them with one blow? Later, Bloody Red commented, "Boy, if it helps his disposition this much, it's a shame he don't come out and kill someone every day!"

He was careful not to be heard, of course. Lucifer's moods were quite predictable—bad and getting worse!

The butchery was intense. No other species was hunted with such vengeance. There was no doubt in anyone's mind that they had better do well with this creature, or the fires of Hell would hold no terrors for them!

These would be the training ground for the real thing when it came along, if, indeed, they weren't the real thing themselves. So that they would not slack off a bit, they simply took it for granted that they were wiping out 'Man'.

Indeed, they acted much like man. When attacked, the males tended to try to protect the females and the little ones. They showed genuine sorrow at the loss of a mate or baby.

To any but the hordes of Hell, their plight would have

wrung tears of blood; but, Lucifer's crew was becoming more evil and hardened, cruel and savage, as the days went by.

There was one exception. A tall, gawky, buck-toothed angel was desperately unhappy with the situation. Upon seeing a little family of the creatures die with their arms around each other in a glade in Eden, his heart ached for days. At times, his heart also ached for the Heaven he had left to come to Earth.

Bucktooth had learned one thing. Since Beelzebub's warning, he didn't even bare his soul to him. Bucktooth didn't have many thoughts, but the ones he had, stayed locked tightly in his own mind. God alone, knew how he felt.

In Heaven, Michael's righteous anger reached the boiling point. "Father, let me spring a surprise attack on him! I promise You, he will never know what hit him!"

If God had given His permission, it would have been hard to tell the warrior angels from Posey. Heaven's angels kept themselves informed daily as to the events on Earth; and all wanted to be in on the fight.

To settle His mighty warrior down, God began to explain what the battle would be like.

"Don't worry about surprising him; My friend, beware that he doesn't surprise you. When the battle comes, it will be here."

Michael possessed the true soldier's mind. The enormity and foolhardiness of such an attack shocked him into momentary silence.

Then, he burst out, "He would have to be a fool to even think of such a thing, let alone try it!"

"Yes, Michael, and a desperate fool at that, but that is what he will be at that time. You have already seen his foolish acts on Earth. To sin was the most foolish thing he ever did. You can't get much more foolish than that.

"If you will notice, he is already showing some signs of desperateness. When he couldn't wipe out all the lesser primates, he discovered that he was less than all powerful—failure was possible. He will become more cunning as time goes on. He will come to the point where more and more, he will be running scared.

"Now," God said, "I have given you food for thought. Don't worry too much, though, for I will add this much more. You will be able to tell when he is about ready to attack."

The history of the tall, beautiful, manlike apes was, indeed, short. Virtually all the primates that were on Earth when he was created would outlive him, even the monstrous Gigantopithicus. Lucifer and his cohorts were nothing if not dedicated.

The minds of the creatures were just not highly developed enough where survival was concerned, to equip them to make it with the powers of Hell, as well as those of Earth, pitted against them. Their minds and bodies had been designed to be a helper to the higher orders of humanity that were to come.

Had everything gone according to the blueprint God had shown the Archangels in Heaven, the more advanced humans would have treated them justly and lovingly. They in turn, would have served with love and loyalty. Basically, they would have performed the more menial tasks. In other words, they were very intelligent beasts of burden.

This being the case, they were not even physically as well adapted to the savage, dog eat dog jungle existence as the lesser primates. They could never survive in competition with them, while being attacked by the vicious carnivores that were turned upon them. Lucifer was driving his followers to attack them with single-mindedness, and his men were driving the carnivores.

In their twilight years, a creature would appear that might have taken the heat off them if it had come upon the scene a little sooner.

This newcomer was strikingly different from the moment of creation on. When the first fallen angel saw one step out of the jungle into a clearing, he knew he was looking at 'Man'. Yes, pre-adamic Man, for sure, and much less intelligent, but he would belong to the genus Homo.

He would not be a three-part being as we are, but he would

have a spirit. He would lack only a true soul similar to ours of being fully human. His simpler soul—simply, his life—would perish at his death.

For the first time, Lucifer's angels found a creature they could not control by mind-bending techniques. God seemed to blend his Spirit with theirs, and cause them to have an instinctive knowledge of good and evil.

Our human would not have won any beauty contest. He had a sloping forehead, great flaring nostrils, and large powerful jaws. What really stood out was his body. It was hairless and smooth limbed compared to the apes. His arms might have been a little longer than ours, but the overall picture was that of 'People'.

When the fallen angels discovered them, they went right to work to destroy them. It was then, to their chagrin, that they discovered they could not control their minds.

Bloody Red turned to his followers. He looked pale and had a sick look on his face as he spoke. "I sure hope someone else gets to Lucifer with this kind of report, before I do. This is really going to cause him to throw a fit."

Indeed, Lucifer did throw a fit. "You worthless bunch of idiots! How could I have been so cursed as to be saddled with such totally inept bunglers?"

After throwing a vicious temper tantrum in the throne room, he again set out to view this newest threat to his realm.

This time, he was not long in finding them. A small band of people were gathering nuts and fruits, when the now invisible horde of Hell's Angels, pre-adamic vintage, arrived.

Lucifer set right out to control their minds. Sitting with his head in his hands in deep concentration, he ordered, "Come Here."

There was a slight stir in the crowd, and then fearing this evil influence, they turned and fled.

Lucifer simply blew up. "Kill them! Kill them!" he shrieked. He raved and cursed God, man, and everyone else who came to his mind.

Death was swift and sure for these hapless creatures, but

Lucifer had done them a favor. We have just seen the first martyrs on Earth.

Having resisted Lucifer, they had resisted sin to the death. God would receive their spirits back to Himself.

Not being true three part humans, their ministry for God would be limited, but they were not to become demons as most of the rest of their race would.

Lucifer settled down a bit, and his mind began to function something like normal again. With the return of thought, he realized his error. With his mind centered in the spirit world as it is, he realized that these people did, indeed, have some kind of spirit. That being the case, he would have to be sure that all had sinned enough that they couldn't return to God at death. If just once, they did something that they knew in their hearts was wrong, he had them.

The shocking order went out: "Not only don't kill these humans, but protect them until we can study the situation in better detail."

As the scene began to unfold on Earth, Jehovah, arose from the throne and beckoned to Michael and Gabriel.

"Come quickly, fellows, we don't have any time to waste. No man must ever see the entire triune God until the work of redemption is complete; however, they can see Me, and those creatures are about to be slain. They have spirits, and those spirits will be arriving here soon."

"In fact," He said, as they hurried out into the outer court, "Michael, you will escort them so Lucifer can't hinder them in route. Alert an entire legion of crack warriors and ready them for immediate transporting.

"Lucifer will be so worked up to start with that you shouldn't have any trouble with this first bunch; however, he will rally quickly. The few more that will die before Lucifer influences them to sin will have to be guarded carefully until you leave the atmosphere of Earth.

"Bring them to the outer court as they will not be allowed in the inner court of the Holy of Holies. There will be a limited ministry for them on the Earth of the future. After the work of regeneration is over, and sin is conquered forever, they will have bodies of spiritual flesh, and be able to be with the Father for eternity. On the other hand, the wicked spirits of Earth will be subject to eternal separation in their disembodied condition.

"You will escort them at legion strength until you are to the outer atmosphere of Earth. Michael, you will then continue on with a small honor guard. The rest of the legion will spread out over the entire Earth. They will be ready to escort any more that are subsequently slain before they sin. Instant transporting to the outer court will take place when you reach the outer atmosphere.

Michael gave a special signal to an angel standing on the outer court wall. The angel, without question, raised the gold encrusted ram's horn trumpet to his lips, and blew a mighty blast. The clarion call echoed and re-echoed throughout Heaven. For the first time ever, Heaven was on Red Alert!

As though out of the very woodwork, the legion commanders began arriving and formed a circle around Michael. "What's happenin' Sar? Air we under attack?" asked a tall redheaded centurion called Calab, while all strained to catch the answer.

Michael waved them to silence, "Raphael, I want The Fighting Seventh Legion in formation and ready to transport immediately. We are going to escort a group of righteous spirits back to Heaven from Earth. You will then bring the spirits of any more people who die sinlessly at Lucifer's bloody hands."

The Seventh cheered, and the rest groaned in disappointment.

The warrior angels assembled in record time. They had tried to shave moments in drill, but this was no drill! This was the real thing, and drill centurions in the future would remind them of what they were capable.

Hardly had they gathered when the Angel of The Lord dropped His hand, and they were gone! They arrived in time to see Lucifer's savage hoods destroy the crowd of beautiful subhumans. Death Angel's features convulsed in anger, and Rafael fitted an arrow into his mighty recurve bow. Big,

Redheaded Caleb, looking like he might just have stepped from the prow of a Viking ship in his horned helmet, gripped his mighty two handed double-edged broadsword until the muscles in his arms stood out in ridges.

Michael was instantly out in front of them with his hands out, palms forward. "Hey you guys! We're not here to fight with Lucifer's angels, and you know it! If my officers aren't under control, how am I supposed to control the entire Fighting Seventh?"

After the warriors had gone, Gabriel turned to the Angel of The Lord and asked, "Lord, I have a question—"

"Yes, I knew you would," cut in the smiling preincarnate Christ. "Ask, My friend, I'm listening."

"My Lord, won't Lucifer sense that there are strange angels in his realm?"

"Ah, indeed he will," returned the Lord, "that is the reason We are going at things this way. If necessary, We will simply blind his angels to our presence. We will make the path of sin as rough as possible. He has a few doubts as to how much We trust him right now, and We intend for him to have a few more!

"Now, Gabriel, hasten and get a welcoming party together. Our guests will be arriving soon."

Lucifer's angels were acting without any effort to conceal themselves; consequently, they were completely visible. Michael's angels were intangible, and thus invisible as they moved in. The mightiest of them took the departing spirits in tow and headed for outer space.

This was a new experience for them in more ways than one. These commando raids were indeed new, but not as new as these soulless spirits. They were a shapeless form without substance. Pure spiritual life, and as the angels found on the way out, they were capable of communication!

"Where are you taking us?" one asked.

The angels were so dumbfounded that for a moment they didn't answer. Then in a compassionate tone of voice, Raphael answered, "Back to Heaven and God."

"Wonderful! That's good," breathed the spirit.

As they neared outerspace, Michael turned to Rafael, "Well, Mr. Legion Commander, the troops are yours. Remember, as much as we hate it, we are not here to fight Lucifer. We're here to protect people. I don't know if I'll be allowed to return. If I don't—man, use your head! See ya—

—with that, he was gone, and the party in the outer court was in full swing.

The spirits immediately recognized the Angel of The Lord and the Holy Spirit as the spiritual force that had controlled them on Earth, and all met in joyful reunion.

The angels gathered around curiously. The nearest thing to them in Heaven was the Father, and He was surrounded by the Shekinah cloud, a cloud so bright it would have destroyed a mortal. How strange, these creatures could be seen, and yet they couldn't. It was almost like looking at a vapor. They were nearly tangible and yet untouchable. There would be very few of them in Heaven.

The three part man of the future would be a saved sinner, and wouldn't be able to come here until after the Crucifixion. Those prior to the time of Christ would have to wait in Abraham's bosom until the risen Christ should take captivity captive and bring them home. He would consist of soul and spirit together. He would be recognizable and nearly tangible. He would look as he had on Earth to those who saw him on the spiritual plane. His two part body would have all the feelings and sensations it had as a three part being.

On Earth, however, there would be myriads of the one part soulless spirits. Folks would call them demons! Yes, and Beelzebub, Lord of the Flies, would be their prince.

In the Inner sanctum in earthly Eden, an unnatural silence reigned. Lucifer sat with his chin on his hand, lost in thought. Finally, Beelzebub voiced one of the questions that was going through Lucifer's mind.

"Master, did those people have spirits, and if they did, where did they go?"

For once, Lucifer didn't try to act perfect and all knowing. He needed Beelzebub's sharp, twisted little mind.

"I'm not sure. It almost seemed that they were transported out of here. However, if that was the case, there were Heaven-based angels here to get them. That doesn't make sense. That would mean that God knows what is going on. If He did, surely, He would try to stop it."

"You don't think they went to Heaven?"

"No, if they did, we would already be under attack. I think that somehow, if they had spirits, they are hiding right here on Earth."

"Well Master, it wouldn't take long to make sure whether the people have spirits or not. We can just influence one to the point that we know he is living in a life of sin, and then kill him. Somehow, they seem to have an instinctive knowledge of right and wrong. We can get one to doing wrong. We'd be ready to collect his spirit if he has one."

"Yes, and outside the body, we should have no trouble controlling the spirit. Having sinned, it would be out of touch with God, and we could move right in."

A new order went out to the realm. "If any person dies for any reason, be sure to find out beyond a doubt if he has a spirit. Use outside influences to force them to kill. Create situations which will cause hatred and anger. Throw the book at them. If you have a good test case, report it. After they start sinning, you should be able to use mind control. If a sinning person hasn't died by that time, we will kill a test case."

As a matter of fact, a number of people who hadn't given in to Lucifer as yet were killed by predators and accidents. However, the Seventh was now functioning like a well-oiled machine. The spirits were whisked away so smoothly that it was still a mystery as to whether they had spirits or not—or even were men at all or some smart, smooth ape.

The Seventh was also getting in some guardian angel experience. They were trying to keep any sinning people from getting killed in order to keep Lucifer in the dark.

"No sinful men have died. However, there is a vicious group

that was just reported. Bloody Red says their leader is so bad that I'd love him, and that he is a super genius compared to the average subhuman. They should make a very good test case. I'll oversee the test myself," Lucifer said.

He didn't expect an answer, and no one gave one.

The tribe was hunting wild game on a flat, grassy plain. This was also the hunting range of a pride of prehistoric killer cats.

Lucifer smiled evilly and mirthlessly in anticipation and satisfaction at the whole setup. These hated men were finished!

To start with, Lucifer didn't even try to control the men. Since they were as deep into sin as they were, he could have; but that would come later. The great cats were not very far away, and on them, Lucifer chose to concentrate.

The huge female raised her head and sniffed the air. Her nose caught the pungent scent of man. Now that didn't seem like too bad an idea for an afternoon snack. With a low growl and a cuff of her paw, she got her family aroused and awake. Alertly, she started her stock, belly flat on the ground and the tip of her tail twitching. The rest followed, not quite so sure about the wisdom of the venture.

The men continued their hunt, apparently unaware of their danger. One thing which Mrs. Cat hadn't noticed was that they were walking in a very exact formation, which the leader had invented. She wouldn't have understood the significance even if she had.

Lucifer nudged Rege, and pointed to the man who was obviously the leader. "Is he big and ugly, or what?"

Rege nodded, "He's Ug-ly! He kinda looks like he might have stolen some ape's head!"

Lucifer only nodded. His attention had turned back to the cats. Things were about to start happening.

When within about a hundred yards of the men, the cats stopped. Mighty hind legs were drawn up under them, hunching and twitching to get in just the right position for the charge. Their ears lay flat, plastered to their heads.

The cats were capable of covering this much distance in a

matter of seconds. The history of this little band of men was about over. The mighty cats, however, were to learn that man had his own chapter to write before they were to dine on fillet of peoples!

As though on command, all the cats sprang into action as one. Long looping bounds ate up the ground.

Almost as though it was a drill, the lead line of men drove the butts of massive, heavy, stone tipped spears into the ground and fell forward in a semi-prone position. The line behind them dropped to a kneeling posture, and held their longer and somewhat lighter lances at ready. Their almost razor sharp points formed a line just above the tips of the heavy spears. Those even farther behind stood boldly with cocked arms, holding their finely balanced javelins at ready.

Ah, yes, following Lucifer's advice was not only bad business for angels and men, it was going to cost a family of cats dearly!

Mrs. Cat reached point blank range, and three javelin throwers launched their weapons. Two found their marks. Two dying cats, out of control, impaled themselves on the large grounded spears.

Alas, the numbers were too great. As each cat struck, the formation was broken up somewhat. At last, penetration was made. When the dust settled, the men were all dead; however, of nine cats, only four would dine on man.

In the excitement of watching the fight, the main purpose of the carnage was nearly forgotten.

Oh, how the Seventh would have loved to be able to slip in and rescue the released spirits, but this they could not do. These men had done that which their spirits bore witness was wrong, and gone the way called the line of least resistance. They had hocked their spirits to the devil, and he had just foreclosed on the mortgage.

Suddenly, Lucifer came alive. "The spirits! The spirits!" Immediately, the fallen angels took the defenseless spirits captive, and brought them back to Lucifer.

A demon had been born! A couple dozen, in fact!

Lucifer stroked his chin as he mused, "So this is 'Man'. I

didn't remember them quite this way, but these are obviously not the same as animals. This has to be our enemy!"

Rege chuckled and pointed, "He's even ugly as a spirit!

Dandy preened himself and added, "Yep, just call him Ug!"

It did not take Lucifer long to appreciate the value of these new additions to his kingdom. Where they were outside their own bodies, he could communicate with them on the spirit level and control them completely.

God would never communicate with them again as creator and friend—only as judge. Thus, the ether waves were quite open. They were so unhappy in their state of eternal separation and as one part beings, that they were obsessed for a body; and they would possess any living creature available.

They preferred another human. When one was found who was evil enough to let them possess him that one became even more a child of Hell!

Now the extermination of the species got into high gear. The evilness of the race seemed to multiply by the square. The more evil the people grew, the more rapid the plunge into total depravity became. Each one that died brought another demon into Lucifer's control.

In one sense, Lucifer had outsmarted himself. With the intelligence and viciousness of the creatures, the age of man was dawning. Instead of becoming extinct, they were gaining in power.

In fact, when this species became extinct, it would not be due to any direct act of Lucifer's. His control, however, was becoming complete. The situation was so well in hand that he actually became about half reasonable to get along with for his lieutenants.

Then the bomb fell. A new man strolled onto the scene. This handsome fellow could have walked up the streets of our modern cities in a business suit, and not looked that much out of place. Modern man would dub him Cro-Magnon man from the relics he left behind, and proudly own him as a forefather.

Lucifer could see nothing handsome about him. In fact,

he took him as a personal affront. He knew that there would only be one true man. If the ones he had been dealing with weren't man in his final form, what in the world were they? Now what was this new dude? He did look much more like what he remembered in the preview he had seen in Heaven, and the final form of man was the one to fear. If the earlier type hadn't had spirits, there would have been no problem. But they did!

Lucifer, the guy that thought he was as smart as God, if not a little smarter, was becoming very confused! And a confused and troubled Lucifer was a creature to be a long ways from if you were within his power! His followers, who thought they had it bad before, found that they hadn't seen anything yet!

The Seventh wouldn't get the chance to escort many spirits from this group to Heaven. Lucifer's experience with the first species had him well equipped to handle this one.

He might not understand the situation, but he had become a past master at engineering the fall of any creature. There would be a number of accidental deaths early on. There would also be a few babies who died before they reached the age of accountability, but his demons and angels would go right to work on the species. The fall of this type would be as swift as it was sure.

These new demons were a delight to Lucifer. They were much more intelligent than those of the less advanced earlier subhumans, except for Ug. If anything, too, they were capable of even deeper depths of evilness. Slacking off on their work became a dangerous past time for the fallen angels. An unseen demon was very apt to be looking on, and word would soon be brought to Lucifer.

On the other hand, the fallen angels outranked the demons, and when they knew one had ratted on them, they poured out their wrath on it. The demons could materialize for a brief period, and the fallen angels would force them to rip each other to shreds before they returned to their former one part status. Thousands of years later in the age of modern man, there would be times when they would materialize briefly and people would call them 'Big Foot' and 'Susquatch'.

The age of man was becoming even more complete now as these new, more intelligent subhumans began to make their presence felt.

Lucifer began to realize that he was losing ground in his battle to bring about the extinction of all the Homo genus. With mounting fury, he began to make existence miserable even for the demons through his mental powers. A good many fallen angels simply lived from day to day, dreading what the morrow would bring.

CHAPTER IX

FISH OR CUT BAIT

As Lucifer's evil followers bullied and murdered their way to positions of elevated rank and esteem in Lucifer's eyes, God prepared to act. Up to this time, Lucifer had selfishly and egotistically pressed forward. He naively believed that God was completely blind to what he was up to.

Hence, there was consternation and no small amount of terror when they heard the golden ram's horn of Heaven echoing throughout every inch of Earth. Even Lucifer paled momentarily before his oversized ego came to his rescue. Surely, God just had some important instructions for them. There was no reason to believe that He was wise to him. He did, however, run out of the temple, and was standing in the outer court when the voice of God was heard.

"Hear Me well, oh Lucifer, all angels, and all demons," proclaimed the thunderous voice of God.

At the mention of the demons, a cold chill ran down Lucifer's spine. The angels virtually grovelled in fear. God knew more than they had given Him credit for. That meant trouble!

There was one tall, gawky, bucktoothed angel who not only wasn't afraid, but was actually delighted to hear the voice of God again. He prepared to concentrate on what God would say—so he would get it all straight.

After a lengthy pause, the voice continued, "You have almost destroyed the beautiful Earth that I have created. The evil you have bred rises as a stench in My nostrils; and I am inclined to destroy the whole sickening mess.

"Since I am a righteous God, I have decided to give you a chance to redeem yourselves. You were created perfect, and have it within your power to do perfect works.

"Correct the damage you have done, and bring about justice, love, and harmony. Reinstall all the righteous laws of nature that I had intended for Earth, and I will forgive your sins. Refuse, and be assured that I will destroy all that is upon the earth. In the end, you will be cast into the Lake of Fire—which, by the way, burns with such hot flames, that they will be blue! Then, you will be banished to the Regions of Nether Gloom, in spiritual torment and separation from God. All your evil desires will mock and torment you for eternity!"

The voice ended, and all became serene again. Birds sang in the trees, and frogs croaked in the marsh. The bugs even hummed as before. But for Lucifer and his followers, it would never be the same again.

If there was ever any indecision on the part of Lucifer, it was not apparent. "Dandy, call the rest of the ranking leaders. Meet me in the inner sanctum." As they approached, he snapped, "Double time!" He was in an unreasoning hurry!

When they all arrived, he got right down to business. His looks were almost pleasant as he began in what was for him a comradely manner.

"Now look, fellas, I remember enough to know that God is not going to wipe out this last bunch of humans. They have too important a part in His unchangeable plan for the future. He's bluffing. He just wants us back under His thumb again!

"I'll have no part of it!" He shouted, slamming a smashing blow of his fist to the table.

The Father of Lies was in high gear and displaying his gift of oratory. Several thousand years later, this gift would be displayed in such men as Adolf Hitler, and later, the Anti-Christ!

He still didn't seem to understand that God could hear,

and knew everything they said. He felt safe within the walls of his inner sanctum.

He stilled the fears of his men, and then sent them out to do the same to all their squads. It is surprising how quickly God's creatures forget His voice. That is, all of them but one forgot. A tall, bucktoothed one was ready to go to work. He didn't quite understand, of course, as usual. He was confident, however, that his friend, Beelzebub, would be able to explain it to him.

Bucktooth found Beelzebub in the outer court. In complete innocence, he approached him as he stood talking to several other ranking angels.

"Beelzebub, when do we'uns start straightenin' this mess out thet God was talkin' 'bout?" he asked in a voice easily heard all over the court. "An' what did He mean, anyways?"

For a moment, squeaky little Beelzebub was speechless. "You got it all wrong, Bucktooth, God didn't mean we had done things wrong. We've just got to do better," he said, when he caught his breath.

Bucktooth would have no part of it. "No Sir-ee, God said everythin' we'uns had did were plumb wrong, an' we'uns better git crackin' or we's goin' ta git destroyed. Ah don't wanna git destroyed. Besides, ah wanna go back ta Heaven. Ah jist don't know where ta start straightenin'."

Fear gripped Beelzebub. This dumb jerk was going to get him in trouble if he didn't get rid of him quickly!

With a knowing look at his friends, Beelzebub answered Bucktooth, not unkindly, "Come on, Pal, I think Lucifer can set you on the right course in all this."

The others grinned at Beelzebub. They too, were sure Lucifer could straighten Bucktooth out.

Without any change of expression, Beelzebub began, "Master, Bucktooth thinks we are supposed to change what we have been doing here; and he wants to go back to Heaven."

Lucifer's voice was low and heavy with menace. "Oh, he does, does he?"

Even slow-witted Bucktooth caught the ominous tone in

Lucifer's voice. However, a courage from somewhere, courage that he had never had before, spurred him on.

"Yes sir! God said ta change thin's, an' the only smart thin' is ta do-ut!"

Lucifer was furious, but held his composure. "You think to tell me what is smart, do you?"

For a while, Lucifer tried to reason Bucktooth out of his obsession. He told him, "Bucktooth, you can't go back to Heaven—you're lost. Everyone on this planet is. You were lost when you left Heaven. And as for changing the creatures here on Earth, it is too late. We can't change them back. They are evil now, and once you are evil, there is no way out. —anyway, God isn't going to destroy Earth. He has gone too far. He loves His humans too much to kill them. He's bluffing."

Bucktooth was adamant. Like many of his mentality, once a fact is grasped, it takes more than smooth oratory, which he doesn't understand anyway, to erase it.

Bucktooth was sure Lucifer didn't understand what God had said. "Sir, yuh don't unnerstand—"

"I? You say I don't unner—ah—understand? Well, see if you can understand this!"

Using his mental, spiritual and physical powers, Lucifer's wrath spilled over on Bucktooth. He put Bucktooth under the influence of such three dimensional anguish as to make purely physical torture seem painless by comparison. When Bucktooth ceased to writhe on the floor, Lucifer ordered, "Drag him out of here! He's dead! Let this be a warning to anyone else who dares to cross me!"

Bucktooth's spirit was lifting toward Heaven, flanked by a squad of shocked and fighting mad warrior angels from the mighty Seventh Legion. As they rose, the voice of God halted them. "Go back, Bucktooth. Return to your body. Your ministry on Earth isn't finished."

After indulging in his sadistic pleasures, Lucifer commented to Dandy and Beelzebub, "The stupid jerk didn't have brains enough to really do us any harm. Now we don't have to worry about him anymore.

"He did give me an idea, though. We will make a pretense of trying to convert these humans. We will give them religion without conversion, and without God. We will teach them of an afterlife, without any spiritual connection, except with us. Let them worship demons as gods. In fact, we can have them worship powerful fallen angels and believe they are worshipping God. Teach them to do rituals and incantations which will give them power with demons. They will even be able to force demons, and maybe even our fallen angels to do their will. Their religion will be strictly in the flesh.

"Give them fancy rituals which do nothing for their spirits. Teach them of a place where they can go through a sort of Hell for a while, and then go to Heaven—earn their way out.

"Let them bury their weapons and prized possessions with their dead—maybe even worship their weapons and pray to them. Let them believe they'll have these possessions in an afterlife, which will be similar to this one. Works! Teach them that they can earn their salvation by their own good works—keeping laws, etc.

"Give them church. Give them priests. Give them colorful ritual with all kinds of different church rulers of different ranks. Give them priests who can act with the power of God, but are my followers. They will believe that their acts have saved them while continuing on in bondage to me.

"As a matter of fact, we can teach at least some of them that after death, they will come back as someone or something else on this Earth."

"Hey! That would really work well, Master. They wouldn't worry too much about doing right in this life, because they'd figure they could do better in the next one!" agreed Beelzebub.

Lucifer looked down his nose contemptuously at the little angel for no apparent reason. A disgusted jerk of his head signaled that the meeting was over.

The angels in the Heavenly throne room writhed in sympathy for Bucktooth as they watched him brought to the doors of death, and heard God intervene. They continued to watch speechlessly, as he was at last dragged out and dumped, unceremoniously, on the ground outside the outer court. They had seen much happen to the mortal creatures on Earth, but this was the first time they had ever seen an angel treated this way.

It was, of course, Gabriel the thinker who finally turned to the throne and asked, "Father, You have intervened in Bucktooth's death, can he earn his salvation in spite of what the others do?"

The Angel of the Lord smiled down upon His brilliant Archangel and asked, "When did he sin to start with, My friend?"

Gabriel looked thoughtful, "I guess I don't know. Going to Earth was not a sin in itself. He is guilty of poor choice in choosing his friends, of course. However, he never succeeded in doing anything that he was ordered to do by Lucifer. To try to be obedient isn't a sin, and I'm sure he never understood that the orders were evil. It appears that he never even knew that Lucifer rebelled. His loyalty to You, now, seems apparent. I Guess I don't know when or even if he sinned."

"I will set your minds at ease, friends, Bucktooth has never sinned! He will be My witness to a dying world. We will never bring judgment without warning. I will use the ignorant to confound the wise! This is only the first time that Lucifer will try to still the voice of one of My witnesses!

"It is true that Bucktooth used poor judgment in the choosing of his friends. Since he wasn't given much judgment, he can't be condemned for not using it. To whom little is given, little is required!

"As a matter of fact, I planned for him to mischoose his friends so he would go to Earth and be My witness.

"He never had the foggiest idea what Lucifer was up to. He really didn't even try to join in on the mind control of the creatures. He simply didn't have the mentality to understand it.

"I will increase his intelligence a little at a time now, as he has need of it.

"Watch closely now, My children, for we are winding down to a deluge, in which everything on Earth will be destroyed—

fish, fowl, and land animals, as well as our subhumans. Everything in which is the breath of life shall die."

"Lord, are You scrubbing Project Earth?" asked Michael.

"No, no!" answered the Lord. "The Earth will lie in a state of ruin for a long period of time. I will then, recreate it in purity. Lucifer will not be the mediator of the new Earth. I, the Angel of the Lord, first under the name Jehovah, then Jesus, will be."

"What about Bucktooth?" Michael asked. "How will he escape Lucifer in the deluge?"

"Ah, My buckos, you two hot heads are going to go get him just before the flood. Remember, Lucifer was created with an inherited rank which he still holds. The two of you are just barely a match for him!"

Outside the outer court on Earth, Bucktooth was just beginning to come back to consciousness. He rolled over and was pleased to see Beelzebub standing there watching him wake up.

Beelzebub's eyes got big, then he muttered, "Looks like he wasn't dead, after all."

Bucktooth's pleasure, however, was short lived. A contemptuous sneer replaced the look of shock on Beelzebub's face. When he began to speak, his voice fairly dripped venom.

"You bumbling, stupid idiot! You're worse than a fool! I don't ever want you near me again! You hear? You're lucky to be alive, and at the rate you are going, you're going to get me killed. From now on, I want no part of you. If I ever see you again, you'll wish Lucifer had you instead! You understand?"

Bucktooth could only nod his head in his anguish. He then dropped it into his hands as Beelzebub spun on his heel and strode away.

After a few more moments, Bucktooth shakily pulled himself to his feet, and shuffled wearily out into the rough country beyond Eden—never to return again.

Bucktooth found himself in a majestically beautiful wilderness area. Ragged, rugged buttes and crags were ripped apart by crystal clear streams and rivers. The rivers raced through canyons, which twisted and darted between the bluffs. The ground would level off, and the streams slow down. This would create small parks which were simply little tiny Edens.

He seated himself beside a small seep spring, which oozed from the bank, and proceeded to do some of the first really deep thinking of his life. Always before, he'd had someone to help him with his decisions. Now, however, he realized he would have to do it himself. Oh! Where and how to start!

Thinking back to what Lucifer had said, he remembered that he had told him it was too late to change the Earth back. God had said to do it, however, so Lucifer had to be lying. He had also said that God was bluffing. That meant that God had said just what he thought He had. Bucktooth didn't believe for a moment that God had, or ever would, bluff. That just wasn't God's way.

After many days of deep thought and soul searching, Bucktooth had it all pretty well figured out. —except for what he should do. He did not know how to pray, since in Heaven, one didn't have to. One spoke face to face. Obviously, Lucifer had never taught anyone how to do it here.

"Master," the demon Ug began, "Bucktooth seems to be content to just simply exist in the wilderness. Do you think I need to keep shadowing him?"

"No. That's about what I expected out of him. After what he went through, he's not going to give me any trouble! We might as well use you somewhere where you are more needed."

After a thoughtful pause, he mused, "I still find it hard to believe he is alive. I could have sworn I sensed his spirit leave his body; but, since we never found his spirit, it probably never quite left him."

With Ug gone, no one witnessed the next chapter in Bucktooth's life. In a moment of extreme anguish, without thinking, Bucktooth cried out, "Oh God, what am ah supposed ta do?"

Instantly, another angel was standing beside him.

Bucktooth cried out in fear, cringing back, and then

shouted joyfully, "Gabriel! Boy am ah ever glad ta see ya!" Then quizzically, he asked, "Man, what air ya doin' down here?"

Gabriel had the chance to do now, what he had yearned to do so many times since Bucktooth entered into his ordeal. He placed his arm around Bucktooth's bony shoulders in a comradely manner, and gave him a sound squeeze. A supernatural strength traveled down Gabriel's fingers and seemed to flow into the frail frame. The back straightened perceptibly.

Gabriel became serious, "You just asked God for instruction. When you speak to God that way, it is called prayer. Do it any time you need anything or when you simply want to communicate with God. I have come to tell you what God would have you do.

"You are God's only witness here on Earth. Since Lucifer won't, you are to take the message to all the subhumans on Earth to straighten up their lives or perish. They are to quit killing each other. They are also to quit killing animals and eating flesh. There will come a time, many thousands of years from now, when eating flesh won't be a sin, but now, it is. They are to repent, cease their evil ways, and be holy. They are to quit lying, stealing, and cheating—that sort of thing. Then the deluge will not come. If they don't change, the Lord will destroy all Earth's life.

Laying his hands upon Bucktooth's head, Gabriel looked up to Heaven and commanded, "In the name of Jehovah God, receive a double portion of courage, and an added measure of knowledge."

As abruptly as he had come, Gabriel was gone. However, he left Bucktooth rejoicing in the Lord.

Ahead of Bucktooth lay a thankless job. The people rejected his preaching in total. In years to come, there would be another creature. He would be a holy man of God whose name was Noah. He would undergo the same thing when he preached that the world was about to be destroyed by another, later flood.

Bucktooth went from tribe to tribe, and person to person warning, "Repent of yer wickedness, an' live yer lives better!"

One hulking subhuman's reaction was typical. He tried to drive his spear into Bucktooth. He was dumbfounded when he couldn't hit him at point blank range. With a deep frown on his almost apelike features, he growled, "Be gone, funny looking man, before I rip you apart with my hands."

Bucktooth's actions were not long in coming to Lucifer's attention. To add to his hardships, the powers of Hell were unleashed against him.

"If Bucktooth goes unchallenged, I'll lose face," Lucifer murmured, as much to himself as to anyone else. I didn't think he'd have guts enough to do something like this after what I did to him." Nodding to himself, he added, "It's time to loose the marines on the scrawny goof!"

Bucktooth noticed a crowd of women pounding seeds on a flat rock. He was just starting to approach them, when it seemed the world was full of Lucifer's angels. To the right and left, and in front and back, he was hemmed in.

For a moment, he was sure all the angels on Earth were there. That old fear that had been such an integral part of him every since he was created, gripped his heart. It seemed to tie it in knots!

Dandy, looking more dangerous than dandy now, snarled, "Where do you think you're going, Stupid?"

Bucktooth knew it was useless to answer. A slight surge of courage, however, gave him the strength to say, "Ah'm goin' ta go witness ta them wimmen over there, when ya git outa mah way."

The dark one's words were, again, more snarl than speech. "Oh, you are, are you? Well, we'll just see about that!"

Remembering his experience back in Eden, Bucktooth almost panicked. The very fact that he had spoken at all, however, seemed to unleash a courage he had never known before. It came straight from the throne of God! By inspiration, he uttered four words, which would come to be greatly feared by Lucifer and all his followers down through time.

"The Lord rebuke you!"

These angels had never heard the words before. Since they were already rebels anyway, they didn't take them seriously. It is said that fools rush where angels fear to tread. These foolish angels all rushed forward one step and stopped. Each face mirrored utter terror as God laid, fear, dread, and horrible pain upon them that would have destroyed a mortal. Each crumpled into a writhing heap. Bucktooth simply walked through them untouched, being careful not to step on anyone.

Never again, would Lucifer's angels frighten Bucktooth so much. To the extent that they did frighten him, he would be able to function with his hair standing on end. He might not have been frightened to start with, had he known the mighty Fighting Seventh Legion and The Royal Charioteers in their flaming chariots of fire were poised to strike had the need arisen. Michael even had the dreaded warrior cherubim with their fiery atomic side arms in reserve.

Bucktooth's spirits were high until he reached the women. He smiled his big toothy grin, and greeted them with: "Howdy, ladies. It's a beautiful day—but God's goin' ta destroy all this here stuff with a big flood ah water, if you'uns don't quit sinnin' and get righteous."

Her features twisted in obvious disgust, one of them said, "What rotten log did that crawl out from under?"

A big hulking, hairy one that made Bucktooth think of the she ape who had made love to Beelzebub, said, "I don't know what you're talking about, but it's our lives. We'll live them to suit ourselves, we'll have you know!

"And anyway, whoever heard of a God? Let alone one that has the power to destroy the Earth? Hasn't it existed forever? It just doesn't make sense.

"Besides, if we are God's creatures, as you have been claiming, He wouldn't destroy us anyway! When you were here the last time, you said God is a God of love, didn't you?"

After the fallen angels returned, Lucifer's face turned even more horrible than ever as he shrieked, "Trash! Idiots! Rejects! O-o-o-oh, what can I think of that will fit you!" He paused as he tried to think what else he could do to strike just as much terror in his troopers' hearts as God had. Even though he couldn't quite measure up, he wasn't doing too bad a job for an amateur.

Depraved though he was, he was no fool. After releasing his venom on them, he said, "I guess we'll have to discard the head on approach, and send out new orders." After pausing to reflect, he continued, "Make life miserable for Bucktooth through a multitude of small happenings.

"Discourage and distract him will be our new tact. Make friends with him. Get his mind off the work that God has for him to do. Convince him that I'm not all that bad a guy after all. Tell him I even worship God—he can tell by the way I quote Him.

"Make him believe there was some sort of mistake. That he is mistaken as to what God wants him to do. Also, try to make him believe the people are all right just as they are—their religion is as good as his; that all religions lead to Heaven, and God is God no matter what name you put on Him. Convince him that his work is complete.

"Beelzebub, renew your friendship with him in order to get close to him. Dissuade him and thus nullify his work."

Sometimes, it pays to be simple. Bucktooth's entire mental make up was simple. In this case, this came to his rescue. Gabriel said he was God's only witness on Earth, period. That meant all the others were wicked and on Lucifer's side. He would have no part of them.

"Sorry, Beelzebub, Gabriel said everybody is plumb evil, but me. All means all! Yuh'll jist have ta go. Ut's jist a simple case ah wickedness an' righteousness. Lucifer brought all this stuff about. The simple fact is, he has ta be every bit as evil as ah ever thought he was."

Now it was Beelzebub's turn to know some remorse. The only creature on this planet that he could really say had ever been his friend, and who actually liked him, was now lost to him forever.

Every stumbling block had an easy answer if you kept it

simple, except one—oh how discouraged he got at times. The subtle demons, even though they couldn't possess him, could certainly oppress him.

He would pour his heart out to the people and be totally rejected. Some imp was sure to be right there to inject a shot of despair and discouragement into his mind.

Again, Bucktooth was too simple for discouragement to last. When forgotten, it was cast aside as he would begin anew, many times over and over, to preach to a lost and dying world.

The word went out in Heaven: "Michael and Gabriel, report to the throne room!"

In a very short time, both angels appeared. All eight of the heavenly Seraphim and both Lion Cherubim were there, but strangely subdued. It was almost like the lull before the storm. They would catch themselves holding their breath, and not know why.

Even Jehovah looked serious. "Well fellows, We are about to test your metal. For the first time, you are going to face Lucifer, head to head.

"Lucifer is about to launch an attack on Bucktooth. He will lead his men, himself. You are to go down and get Bucktooth, before the destruction of Earth.

"The Seventh, the Charioteers, and the Warrior Cherubim will be backing you up. They won't be visible to Lucifer, because we will blind his forces to them. They will approach after he has materialized. They are there solely to nullify the troops he has with him, if necessary. You are to handle Lucifer, yourselves.

"As you return, bring our troops with you. Their ministry is finished as soon as you leave. They won't be needed again until after the flood is over."

Even as God was speaking, Bucktooth was reasoning his heart out with some very uninterested folk in a primitive human camp back on Earth.

Smoke and flame flashed before his eyes. Lucifer stepped

from the flames as he made his melodramatic appearance with a large contingent of his followers at his back.

"Run!" an old woman screamed, "The end really has come; just like he said!"

Bucktooth's heart simply melted within him. The fallen angels were one thing, but Lucifer was quite another. Even Michael and Gabriel would know a portion of fear when they confronted him; and Bucktooth certainly wasn't on a par with them. Terror overwhelmed him; however, in his fright, he did what was becoming second nature to him—he prayed!

"Lord help me!" he cried as he dropped to his knees.

A gasp rippled through the assembled angels. Even in his terror, Bucktooth looked up. Standing between him and Lucifer, Bucktooth recognized two mighty angels from Heaven: Michael and Gabriel!

The element of surprise went to the two holy angels, but it only helped momentarily.

Lucifer's words were like bullets. "What do you want? This is my jurisdiction. I'm in charge here."

Apollyon and Beelzebub stepped up by his side as he spoke.

Instead of two to one, it was now three to two. Behind them stood Rege and Dandy. The hair on Gabriel's neck seemed to be standing on end. He hoped no one noticed.

If Michael was afraid, Gabriel couldn't tell it. Gabriel started to speak, and was somewhat surprised to hear his own voice. He couldn't help thinking he sounded much cooler than he felt.

"We have come to take Bucktooth back to Heaven. God is ready to rain destruction upon Earth. Bucktooth, alone, is not deserving of punishment! The rest of you richly deserve the Earth that is about to be your home."

Lucifer snarled back, "You can't take him with you. He's a sinner. He didn't convert a single soul here. He's been trying for over a year. No one has listened to him. His works were not only second-rate, but you can't show me one place where he is even average, let alone perfect!"

Lucifer was already showing what he would be like as Satan the Accuser.

Gabriel replied instantly, "Bucktooth never once sinned. Not one thing that you ordered him to do has he even made a genuine try at. Even if he had tried, he didn't know you were in rebellion, and would have been obeying you as a representative of God. Where there is no law, there is no transgression!"

With an arrogant thrust of his jaw, Lucifer turned Satan gritted out, "We'll just see if you take him or not!"

All three moved forward menacingly. Rege and Dandy had been in on the first attack on Bucktooth, and they wisely, held back.

Bucktooth hid his eyes. Whatever was going to happen, he really didn't want to see.

For the first time, Michael spoke. Those four little words that Bucktooth had used on the fallen angels would be used again, only on bigger game. "The Lord rebuke you!"

The three had no intention of stopping. It was going to take more than a few words to stop them!

In mid stride, Apollyon and Beelzebub, as well as all the angels behind them, crumpled in a writhing heap.

Satan thought he had a great deal of mental and spiritual power, but he hadn't seen anything yet. An unseen power seemed to raise him up on tip toe. His eyes bulged, as though they were being gouged out. There was horrible intense pain behind them. His tongue already protruded from his mouth and was beginning to swell as though he were dying of thirst in the desert. He looked for all the world like a man that is being strangled slowly. Panic gripped him as he struggled for air. His heart pounded until it hurt in spasms of horrible pain.

From now on, he would know how someone dying of a heart attack felt. His whole body tingled as if the circulation had been shut off, and was just starting up again. His head ached with a mighty migraine headache. There was no part of his body that didn't hurt horribly. Even his teeth ached.

It felt as if he had a rope around his neck; and someone up there was lifting him off the ground by it. In fact, it felt as if his feet were stuck to the ground and his head was being pulled from his body, slowly. His body felt as if it were being torn apart in all directions at once.

He thought, distractedly, that God must be causing all the pain he had ever inflicted on others to come upon him in a moment of time. "I didn't even hurt old Bucktooth this much," he thought.

It is beyond human comprehension or description, to understand the forces that were driving his spirit to the very edge of, but not quite past the point of extinction.

God removed His power, and Apollyon and Beelzebub, as well as the rest of the angels, would have to be carried away. Beelzebub and Apollyon were conscious. The rest weren't. Satan seemed to be staring into space as he shouted "Ug! Where are you? Get over here!"

"I'm right here, Sir," the big, ugly demon replied.

Satan looked to one side and said, "Oh—OK. Go get some help to drag these jerks away."

Satan managed to leave under his own power, but never again would he take on God, one on one. Even when he attacked Heaven, he would have all his forces at his back.

After Satan left, Michael and Gabriel helped Bucktooth to his feet. All hugged each other in glee.

They began ascending slowly. The people in the subhuman camp watched them in amazement until they were obscured by the clouds. Then, in an atomic instant of time, literally, at the speed of thought, all were standing in the Holy Place in Heaven. The Angel of the Lord, and ten rejoicing creatures joined in the celebration which his Witness and two mighty lieutenants had begun on Earth. The warrior angels, too, were glad to be home from their tour of duty. Bucktooth summed it up with, "Home, sweet home!"

CHAPTER X

THE DELUGE AND WAR

An exception was being made in Heaven. Normally, only angels of the highest rank were allowed in the throne room. After what he had gone through, the Lord felt that Bucktooth had earned the opportunity to enter the Holy of Holies, and watch the destruction of Earth. Time was running out for the creatures there.

Bucktooth had been home for nearly seven days. The memory of his rescue from the clutches of Satan still crowded almost everything else from his mind.

Satan, on the other hand, was beginning to strut and crow, "I told you God wouldn't destroy the Earth. He's trying to figure out how to save His precious people without having to pardon us, and let us go our own way."

Beelzebub squeaked, "You sure are smart, Master. It looks like God is going to have to live with the fact that some of His creatures are going to live as they wish to whether He likes it or not."

Satan swelled with pride as he boasted, "Yes, and not only that, in time, I'll rule in Heaven. From the first time I walked into the Holy of Holies, I wanted that place for myself. That throne will sure feel good! There will be no one who outranks me. Then watch that pair of bootlickers who thought they were so smart when they came down here. They had no right to muscle in on my territory and take over!"

Outside the Temple, the sky was turning dark and lowering. A guard angel by the door looked apprehensively at the tumbling clouds. "Do you suppose we should warn Lucifer?" he asked.

"He said he would skin anyone who disturbed him, remember?" answered the guard on the other side of the door. "Anyway, what would you say? He's seen storms before. They really don't bother him."

The first guard just shrugged and prepared to get wet.

The walls of the temple were so thick that Satan couldn't hear the thunder that had ceased to roll and was cracking like the report of monstrous artillery pieces being fired in salvos. The seventh day was drawing to a close!

He didn't know that anything was amiss until a volcano some thirty miles away blew its top. The force of the blast was away from the temple; however, the floor seemed to rise several feet before falling away twice as much.

Everyone tumbled out to see what was happening. All had seen volcanos, but that had been some time ago. It had been even longer since they had seen one this close. Lava, ash, and poisonous gas were shooting into the air as though coming from the throat of a large, and very sick monster. They viewed it only briefly; however, for the sky seemed to open up, and rain fell in a cloud burst. They rushed back into the temple, which had withstood the first quake, thanks to the divine architectural plan.

No sooner had they gotten in, than another quake struck. This one was designed to bring down the blasphemously used temple. It fell in rubble about them, and there was nothing to do but take the storm on the chin.

All mortal life was racing to higher ground, or clinging to floating debris. Those who were struggling to reach higher ground were becoming progressively more sluggish as the poisonous gases from the volcanos made the air more and more unbreathable.

Long before the tops of the mountains were covered, all land based life was destroyed by the volcanic action and the water.

Marine life would take a little longer. The oxygen in the

water had to be used up and the poisonous gases absorbed before the fish died in agony, in schools, fins erect and mouths gaping.

Tsunami tidal movements would bury them deep, laying layers of sediments with each movement. The more primitive would die first and be buried deepest. The more advanced would die last, and be in the upper layers of sediments.

Layers would only be approximately in the same order. Bones would be mute evidence to warn later types of life. They, alas, would try to use them to prove Satan's lies.

The time would come when all creatures in whose nostrils was the breath of life would be dead. The Earth would be a desolation, destruction, and an empty waste—without form and void.

God had wrecked judgment, but in sorrow. He received no satisfaction from His actions.

Had it been possible for angels to weep in sorrow, tears would have flowed around the great crystal screen. As it was, they all embraced in loving fellowship, sharing their anguish. All of Heaven's music ceased for the time being, and never will be heard on Earth until the entire work of redemption is complete.

Bucktooth moaned, "Oh, if they'd jist ah listened—ah tried, oh how ah tried! Maybe if ah'd tried harder—"

"Hey! None of that!" said Gabriel. "You did everything you could. They had their chance, and rejected it. Now they have to pay for their sin. You mustn't blame yourself!"

The storms of Earth ended, and the waters that covered it were more a caustic soup than water. Its sun ceased to shine—even its orbit had changed. God would control Earth's interior heat and keep it high enough that it wouldn't completely freeze up; however, it certainly experienced an ice age without a great deal of open water.

The high spirits of Satan and his followers really took a nose dive. They now, had nothing to do but levitate above the water, or sit on the ice. They could always vent their evil dispositions upon one another when they got bored.

Satan realized he needed something to occupy his troops, and a plan was born. He would attack Heaven!

The military mind of Michael was also at work. If Satan were going to attack, what better time could he find? The warrior angels were on limited alert, and everyone else was getting a taste of military training. If it came to a fight, every angel of every rank and training would be involved. Even Bucktooth and the flower waterer underwent training.

Satan's cold evil eyes spanned his lieutenants, and his mouth formed a thin line of a slit in his face as he prepared to speak. "I'm not about to stay down here and rot in this chaotic mess. It is about time to attack and take over in Heaven! We'll make 'em wish they had never tangled with us!"

In spite of his love of a good fight, Apollyon asked, "Master, what chance do we stand, outnumbered two to one?"

Satan's expression mellowed slightly, as it always did, when he prepared to answer his favorite aide. "You forget the demons, by friend. They can materialize long enough to fight, and will go a long ways toward evening up the odds."

Now it was Beelzebub's turn to question, "How are we going to get up there so we can fight, Master? God sure isn't going to transport us up there to attack Him, is He?"

Satan answered patently, which was unusual when he spoke to Beelzebub. "We'll levitate if we have to. Even though we have stayed here on Earth, God made the universe our playground, so to speak. I think we can travel at nearly the speed of thought. It probably won't be as fast as God did it, but it shouldn't take long. Anyway, it sure beats hanging around here."

Again, Apollyon asked, "What if we are attacked in route?"

"So much the better," said Satan. "We would be fighting on neutral ground that way.

"Now call your men and have them ready to march as soon as possible!"

The news ricochetted around the earth like some kind of crazy bullet. Within twenty-four hours, the mighty army that had stood on the plain in Heaven was reassembled around

Satan. And this time, it was swelled by the multitude of demons who were at Satan's beck and call.

It was a formidable army indeed! Their trip would be less than instantaneous, but it would be quick enough that it was well Michael was ready.

God, Himself, sounded the alarm. Michael was in the throne room at the time. God said, "Michael, Lucifer is on his way." The Archangel left so quickly that it would have been disrespectful under any other circumstance. God understood His mighty angel very well, however.

"Red Alert! Battle Stations!" Michael shouted to the sentinel on the wall. His waving arms demonstrated his excitement.

There was an urgency in the air that left no doubt in anyone's mind. This was no drill! There was plenty of time, but there was none to waste. He gave last minute orders, and then even had time for dread.

Suddenly, they were in sight! The sky over Heaven was full of the evil creatures.

God, as the Angel of the Lord, struck the first and probably the most telling blow. He stepped forth and commanded, "Demons, in the name of Jehovah God, your creator, you are commanded to return to Earth!"

In the presence of their creator, they could do nothing but obey. Satan was a lesser being and of lesser rank—and rank was what they understood.

Satan knew a moment of sinking sensation within himself at this, then pure fury took over. He felt that the evil character of his followers would give them an advantage over the righteous angels of Heaven. He had, however, overlooked the fact that when they went into a life of sin, they began to deteriorate. They were not even close to the righteous angels in strength and power.

When Bucktooth returned to Heaven, there was one vacuum. He needed a friend to replace Beelzebub. It was only natural that he gravitate to one of something like his level of mentality and skill. Posey, the flower waterer, was just right.

As on Earth, Bucktooth wasn't given any specific orders, and neither was Posey. The two friends, one six-foot six, skinny, and gawky, and the other five foot two and weighing twice as much as Bucktooth, were standing looking up into the sky at the descending horde.

"Posey, ah'm scairt!" Bucktooth said in a quivery voice.

"Yah, me too!"

"Yah, Posey, but ya'all ain't had Lucifer shaking ya loose from yer life!"

"Now, ah'm even more skairt!" Posey answered in a voice just as quivery as Bucktooth's.

The fallen angels approached ground level, and a cowering Posey whimpered, "Boy! They shore do look awful!"

"They air awful. Think what ut'll be like if'n they win."

Posey's eyes held a look of desperation. "Ya know somptin' Pal? We'uns better fight!"

"Yep," said Bucktooth. "Ah'm skairt to, an' ah'm skairt not to. Ah guess we'uns better do-ut!"

"Ya remember how Michael was tellin' us ta' fight standin' back ta' back so's we can pertict each another?" asked Posey

"Yah, but ya'all can only pertict the bottom half ah me," Bucktooth said with a grin.

For a moment, Posey forgot to be scared. "Don't get sassy. If'n ya wasn't so tall an' skinny, there wouldn't be so much stickin' up in the way. An' anyhow, who's goin' ta pertict the part ah me what sticks out on bof sides?"

Satan was close now, and the two unlikely warriors quit joking and began trying to figure out what to do.

Immortal beings were locked in mortal combat! The battle progressed on every plane and dimension; mental, spiritual, and physical. Except for those who had witnessed the attack on Bucktooth, none had ever seen an angel die before. Now, a steady stream of heaven's angels' spirits were making their way to the River of Life and the trees of life which lined its banks. The whole area was guarded by the mighty warrior cherubim. A mere sip of water or bite of fruit put them back in their spiritual bodies. A wall of flaming swordpoints met any fallen angel who attempted to reach it. These would turn back, and begin a sad return trip to Earth. They would never be angels again. Now they were disembodied spirits; demons just as the dead from Earth were.

Mighty Caleb was standing with his back to a wall. Beelzebub, Rege, and Dandy prepared to attack him simultaneously. Caleb missed Beelzebub's head by an inch when he swung his mighty broadsword at him. Beelzebub jumped back far enough to be out of position. With Caleb out of balance, Rege thought he saw an opening. He stepped in behind the swinging sword only to have Caleb bring the sword in backwards, butt first. Caleb's fist and the hilt of the sword went clear out of sight in Rege's stomach. This didn't do any permanent damage, but Rege's face went from purple to green around his white, bloodless lips, which formed a perfect O in the center of his face. That was enough for Rege. There just had to be an easier way!

Beelzebub attacked again with Dandy right behind him. Caleb took advantage of his height and Beelzebub's shortness to kick him right on the point of the chin with a steel shod foot.

Beelzebub went 'night-night'. With the deftness of a scribe with a pen, Caleb swung the mighty broadsword and Dandy's head rolled from his body. He wouldn't be needing his mirror anymore!

Bucktooth and Posey were present, but that is about all that could be said for them. They were spending most of their time trying to get out of harms way—not very successfully.

Bucktooth looked up, and his heart sank. Apollyon!

Apollyon noticed Bucktooth at almost the same instant. He actually roared, and called Bucktooth some very uncomplimentary names as he came in a rush.

"You scrawny creep! This is all your fault!" he said unreasonably.

Apollyon picked both Bucktooth and Posey up, one in each hand. He grasped them by their robe fronts, and was about to bang their heads together when a pleasant voice asked,

"Apollyon—have you slipped so far that you pick on guys like these to fight? I thought you were big and tough."

Before even looking to see who had spoken, Apollyon threw the two frightened angels away like discarded trash. He was surprised to find himself facing an angel at least as big and muscular as himself. This guy might be a challenge. He couldn't remember the dude, but aside from Satan, he feared nothing. A little discretion; however, would probably have stood him in good stead.

"You seem to know me, which is natural; however, I can't be expected to know every second rate angel in Heaven. Before we fight, who am I to say I thrashed?"

"I have no name as such, only rank and position. Jehovah calls me 'The Death Angel'. My

friends, which definitely leaves you out, call me DA. After I get through with you, you will doubtlessly call me many things."

Apollyon's ego was such that he didn't heed the warning DA offered. Choosing to fight on the physical plane, Apollyon attempted to drop kick DA with both feet. DA sidestepped easily, and Apollyon never even came close. Instead of being forewarned, Apollyon was furious. He hit his feet in a bound.

DA was through fooling round, and he hit the rising Apollyon on the point of the chin with an overhand right.

Groggily, Apollyon wondered why he was still on the ground, when he could distinctly remember just getting up.

"Sock-ut to 'im, DA!" shrieked Bucktooth, his own arms windmilling. His fist grazed Posey's cheek, but the fat little angel never even noticed in his excitement.

DA was standing waiting for him to get up again. The sportsmanship infuriated Apollyon enough to clear his head. When he got up this time, however, it wasn't nearly as smooth and quick a move as before. Still acting stunned, he wabbled toward DA, and then lashed out, striking him in the stomach, just under the floating ribs.

DA doubled up, and Apollyon brought the side of his hand down on the back of his neck at the base of the skull.

DA drove his face into the ground, and rolled aside.

Apollyon landed where he had been. DA kicked Apollyon on the side of the head—hard—and rolled to his feet.

Apollyon kicked DA's feet out from under him, and when he lit beside of the fallen angel, Apollyon got a head lock on him as they struggled to their feet.

Apollyon had seen some strong angels, but DA was something else. DA arched his back, stamped on Apollyon's instep to get a little slack, and simply pulled his head out of the hold. The way they felt, he wasn't sure he had any ears left. Apollyon stood there looking shocked for a moment. DA took advantage of his surprise to throw a combination of punches which dropped Apollyon on his face.

Apollyon was anything but a quitter. He lit on a stout branch and came up swinging. DA ducked the first swing and then caught the club across his forehead on the backswing as he raised his head. He dropped like a felled ox, and lay still for a few moments.

Apollyon had enough of this fight anyway, and could leave now with honor—claiming victory.

DA recovered his wits in moments and arose to continue the conflict. He saw Apollyon leaving and assumed he was beaten. For thousands of years, both would claim victory. Both awaited only the opportunity for a rematch. This would come when Apollyon became too vicious to be allowed to remain loose on Earth. DA would not only win, but place Apollyon in Tartarus, Hell's maximum security prison. There he would rule as Satan's second in command in Hell, a place Satan would seldom if ever visit until God, Himself, chains him there during the millennium.

Satan's angels were a poor match and outnumbered. It soon became plain how the contest would end. Heaven's angels were defending their home, and fought desperately. Satan's angels were soon wishing they had stayed in their own home to start with. Many were in full retreat to the primeval soup of Earth.

As more and more died, or just quit and fled, the battle became more intense for those who stayed. It dwindled down to Satan, Apollyon, and Beelzebub. Beelzebub couldn't take any more, and headed for home.

Tough though Apollyon was, and he looked the part now after the beating his face had received from DA, there was just so much he could stand. At last, he too reached the point where he could take no more, and fled.

Satan fought on. No angel or number of angels was his match, and he didn't seem to know how to quit. At last, Jehovah approached the conflict and ordered, "That's enough, fellas. Everyone stand back."

Satan was triumphant and sneering. "I have fought You to a draw. Now will You compromise with me?"

Jehovah looked at him sadly, "I cannot, nor will not compromise with anyone, Lucifer. You were a loser from the moment the first thought to rebel entered your heart!"

Satan started to bristle; and at that moment, Jehovah waved His arm and commanded, "Be gone!"

God did not transport him instantly. Rather, He gave him a taste of real power such as he had never even dreamed of. It seemed he was picked up bodily and flung into space. It was as if a powder charge had been detonated under him and he left like some kind of projectile. To those waiting on Earth, he struck the atmosphere with the appearance of lightening.

Michael, Gabriel, and DA gathered around Jehovah, and Gabriel asked, "DA! What happened to you?"

"Oh, I just whipped Apollyon is all."

"You better get to the Tree of Life and eat some of its healing leaves," said Michael. "You're a mess!"

"Yah, I know, but I kinda hate to. You know what I mean? I'm kinda proud of my wounds and the way I got them."

Jehovah nodded reflectively and spoke, "Yes, DA, I do know what you mean. As Jesus, I shall receive wounds in the course of saving mankind, and I will retain the scars like medals of honor. Go your way. I give you the same privilege."

DA went to the Tree of Life and returned munching on a handful of leaves. Bucktooth and Posey had joined Michael and Gabriel. The Angel of the Lord, in the mean time, had left to rejoice with and congratulate the rest of His army.

Michael looked DA over approvingly. "Boy! You look sharp!"

The big angel's ears were cauliflowered, and a slight scar ran at an angle across his forehead, where the club struck him. The result added to the handsome angel's rugged good looks.

A contrite Bucktooth said, "Man, ah'm shore sorry ya had ta git all messed up fer us, DA."

"I didn't get messed up just for you, Bucktooth. I got messed up for all of us and for Heaven itself. As a matter of fact, I have been spoiling for a fight with him ever since he has been doing all the terrible things on Earth that he has. The pleasure was all mine!"

The big angel smiled crookedly, and patted both misfits on the back as he spoke.

If he had been thought a harsh master before, Satan's followers would find him almost unbearable now. And the Earth was destined to remain in this wasted state for several thousands of years; with no one knowing if this stage would ever end or not.

Project Man might have been scrubbed and this planet turned into their prison forever, for all they knew.

CHAPTER XI

THE RECREATION AND THE FALL

Over the long period of time that the Earth had lain waste, every vestige of life that had gone on before had been wiped clean, except for the bones that would form fossils for later man to study. The air gradually purified itself. Slowly, the water followed suit.

Now, the water would again support life. A very dreary, dark place it was though. The air was so full of water vapor that it hung in a constant fog. The sky could not be seen. The surface was simply one vast ocean, the Earth's divinely controlled internal temperature with the blanket of vapor having melted the ice.

Boredom was the name of the game for the captive fallen angels and demons. Hence, there was no small stir when an angel raced up to Satan and said, "Master! Master! The Spirit of God is moving upon the face of the waters!"

Soon the omnipresent Spirit encompassed the Earth. The demons were terrified. The fallen angels were not much better off. This was a new experience for them too. Sure, the Holy Spirit is everywhere, all the time, but this was an almost tangible presence. They could feel Him! He seemed to be brooding, almost pensive!

Suddenly, as though He wished to see better, the order rang out, "Let there be light!" Instantly, it was like a huge switch had been thrown and the lights came on as the Shekinah glory of the Father enveloped the Earth.

For twenty-four hours, the light was battling valiantly to penetrate the heavy fog. The light was very good, but the fog was very thick.

Now, as though trying to see more, God ordered, "Let there be an expanse between the moisture of the clouds and the sea." Now visibility became good under a solid overcast sky.

During the rest of the twenty-four-hour period, God contented Himself by merely cruising around the Earth. His very presence seemed to hallow it in spite of the evil creatures who cowered at His approach. They had tangled with Him once. It would be a long time before they became desperate enough to try it again.

It would seem the solid expanse of water became depressing even to God. At His order, the large land masses raised up out of the water; which, cascaded into the hollows, forming lakes and seas. The valleys and canyons were cut into the soft earth as the continents arose, causing the water to cascade back to the seas.

This third day dawned even busier than the first two. The muddy, soggy earth dried out under the loving breath of the Father. At the end of the twenty-four hours, He had recreated all the plant life that had died out in the deluge.

At the end of the day, He looked over His handy work and found it perfect, very good indeed!

Up to this point, the light had been supplied by the Shekinah glory of God. Now, He was ready to turn it over to natural means. As the fourth day started out, He ordered, "Let there be lights in the heavens!"

The cloud cover broke up, and the beautiful starlight burst forth upon the Earth.

The Earth wasn't close to any star. Now God created a new sun and moon. He created the sun so exactly the right size and distance from Earth that life could be supported on the purified planet.

The slightest error would have destroyed life instead of supporting it; but God is perfect. He can make no error! Earth fell into its new orbit around its custom-built sun, and the moon began orbiting the Earth. A semblance of normalcy settled upon the new system.

The fifth day would be another busy one as God recreated every living thing in the animal kingdom except man. There would be one big difference in them. Unless killed, they would live forever. Also, there would be no accidental killings, their death would have to be intensional.

The recreation of the animals had been a word of mouth thing. Now on the sixth day, God began His masterpiece—the one Lucifer had dreaded so much—Man!

Adam, He created by hand, and with loving attention to every detail. He was formed and molded out of red earth, and was always a red, ruddy individual.

The body was finished now, but as of yet, that was all it was. He was like a corpse lying on a slab. God would have to give mouth to mouth resuscitation! He breathed into him the breath of lives! When He did so, Adam received his spirit and became a living soul.

Man was a three-part being, just as God was. His body would relate to Jehovah, who is and was, the body portion of the Godhead. Adam's spirit related to the Father, the Spirit of the Godhead. And his soul related to the Holy Ghost—the soul of the Godhead.

The only difference would be that God could split up the Godhead, with each part going places and doing things as the need arose. On the other hand, if that happened to Adam, he would die.

Time was running short, and Adam had hardly stretched his limbs when the greatest parade ever witnessed began to pass by: the entire animal kingdom! Adam named each in its turn.

One type was noticeable for its absence. There were no subhumans to help Adam with his work. God, foreknowing what havoc Satan would wreck on this Earth, wisely, did not recreate these species. There were also certain other animals which would not be able to survive in the new environment that the Earth would have. These, He also left out.

Instead of giving the sub-humans to Adam as helpers,

God caused a deep sleep to fall upon him. He took out one of his ribs, closed the wound, and healed it. God, then, made his wife out of the rib. She became his help mate. He awoke with a beautiful, smiling young lady holding his head—welcoming him back to the world of reality.

God placed them eastward in Eden in a beautiful garden. They were busy, for they not only had to take care of the garden, but God went right to work to educate the pair. By the time of the fall, they had an education that can't be duplicated today! In the future, they would wear skins, but dumb cave men they weren't!

The seventh day began, and God rested. Never until redeemed man enters eternity, will He create anything more. His Sabbath will last until He creates the New Heaven and the New Earth.

When the work of creation ceased, Satan began to stir. He called all his lieutenants together. No temple would he have now, and Eden was a good place to be from—a long ways from! Satan was now an outcast where once he had reigned—ah—the price of sin!

"Look, you bums," he said, "lay low. We don't want these people tipped off to us. I'll study them in disguise or invisibly. I'll figure out their weak points. I'll handle this all myself. We can't afford to lose this opportunity. If we get one that is probably all we'll get."

Satan made himself invisible, and entered the garden stealthily. The righteous spirits that he had missed before the flood were around and some invisible Heavenly angels as well. Since they too, were all in their immaterial form, they would be able to detect him if he wasn't careful.

It did not take him long to discover that God had created the Tree of Knowledge of Good and Evil. Of course, the man and his wife had been forbidden to eat of it. It had only been planted to test them. Since this was the only sin they were capable of committing, this would have to be his area of attack.

Satan displayed an amount of patience that was completely absent when he was the despotic ruler of the earlier Earth.

In fact, he took many years, simply studying the couple and every aspect of the task of bringing about their fall. If he failed once, he might never succeed. And this being the case, he was taking no chances.

The animals God recreated behaved as He had intended the first ones to. The fallen angels and demons chafed, but behaved themselves. Satan had spoken, and the way he had spoken left no doubt in their minds. If they blew it, and caused him to fail in his plan for the fall of man, their future would be grim indeed.

The final and most difficult part of his plan was the actual communication—the contact. How was he to do this without blowing his cover?

Their very innocence might be the answer. Adam appeared to be a little too sharp. He would work on Eve, not because she was a woman, but because she wasn't quite as smart as Adam.

Now he had to choose the vehicle. Since Adam and Eve were the only ones in the garden who could speak, this would be somewhat of a problem. Eve would just have to get used to an animal that could talk.

Even as innocent as she was, if he appeared in human form or as an angel, and tried to deceive her, she wouldn't buy it.

Finding an animal that he could use was also something of a problem; for just the use of mind control wouldn't do. He would have to possess the animal the same way the demons did in order to be able to speak through it. He would have to be able to use its body just as he would his own.

Eve seemed to adore a gorgeous stag that frolicked in the garden. Satan was sure she would love it, if he could speak to her. When he exerted his mind control on the beast, however, it showed signs of distress. When he tried to possess it, it resisted to the extent that he was afraid it would kill itself. At last, he had to release it.

Satan was furious, but could not afford a temper tantrum now.

While pondering his problem, a slender flying reptile lit

close by. It perched with its long, slim legs delicately clutching a limb.

"Ah," thought Satan, "just the kind of creature a woman would be attracted to. He is pure beauty."

Exerting some mind control on him, he met no resistance whatsoever. The creature seemed to release himself readily to being possessed. In short order, he was totally the extension of Satan's will.

Satan was careful not to cause the reptile to speak except when Eve was alone, and she never thought to mention it to Adam. Of course, speech would have been impossible for the animal on the physical level, but Satan could use his own eyes, ears, and throat from within it.

After her initial surprise, Eve came to like this beautiful and talkative animal. It was nice to have someone beside Adam and God to speak to. Soon she was even sharing little harmless secrets with it. The thought of it betraying her never entered her mind. Why, it was almost like having a best friend!

One day, while seeming to wander aimlessly, Satan worked her around until he had her under the deadly tree. The serpent perched right in a cluster of the tempting fruit, then asked, "God allows you to eat anything you want in the garden, doesn't He?"

"Everything except the fruit of that tree you are in right now. He says we shouldn't even touch that fruit, lest we be tempted to eat it and die."

The Serpent scoffed, "Oh pooh! It won't kill you. It's not poison." So saying, he took a big bite and swallowed it as his beady eyes lit up with pleasure.

"God just knows that if you eat it, you will be as smart as He is. You'll actually be like a god."

One thing was for sure, the serpent didn't shrivel up and die. In fact, he looked, if anything, even more healthy than he did before. You could tell he was smart too, couldn't he talk? And some of the things he said were surprising, coming from an animal.

Eve reached up, but stopped short. She reached again, and this time, she actually picked some of the luscious fruit, and turned it over in her hand. She watched the dew drops sparkle on it.

Satan watched with bated breath. He knew better than to push her now. All he could do was wait.

Two, then three times, she started to take a bite and dropped her hand. Finally, just a nibble, and then she took a bite and swallowed it! Horror distorted her face as the import of her act set in. Her first sin after eating the fruit was akin to Satan's first one. Selfishness! She would have to get Adam to eat too, or she would be alone—if she didn't die, and she didn't even feel sick. Maybe the serpent was right, after all.

Adam picked this unfortunate moment to walk up and see what she had done.

"Oh eat some, Honey. It won't kill you—and you'll be so smart!"

Adam looked at her in silence. Already, he could see the change in her, but what would life be like without her? He could well remember his life before God created her. No Thanks!

The moment he harbored this thought, he gave Satan the opening he needed. He brought all the mind control powers he had to bear. Adam too, hesitated, reached and ate. Worse yet, he did it knowing full well what he was doing!

The two fallen humans hugged each other and shivered in the cold. The first tears they had ever shed were cruising down their cheeks. Racking sobs shook them. How could they have been so dumb?

What would God say? Worse yet, what would He do? Did the future hold anything for them? Would they really die? Could God ever forgive them?

Ah, the price of sin. They were so miserable!

—and their nakedness! It seemed their very soul as well as body lay bare for the world to see. Now the bodies which had been so beautiful before they sinned, were symbolic of the sin within them. From now on, these beautiful bodies would have to be covered to show that God had covered their sin. It would not be because their flesh was evil, or any less beautiful, it would be because their flesh was symbolic of sin. Eve gathered some large fig leaves, and using some light vine, stitched them together to make aprons for them. This helped their feelings, but really didn't do a lot to cover them. The leaves began to dry, shrink, and get brittle immediately. The stitches tore out easily.

Oh, how they dreaded for God to show up in the garden, as they knew He would later on that evening. Like frightened rabbits, they searched for warrens in the brush to hide in as the time drew nearer.

All too soon, they could hear God calling, "Adam! Adam! Where are you?"

Adam realized he could remain hidden from God no longer, and answered, "Here I am, Lord. I was afraid and hid, for I knew I was naked, and I knew You could look into the very center of my soul!"

"Who told you, you were naked? Have you eaten of the forbidden tree?" asked God.

"The woman that You gave me, gave me some, and I did eat." Adam said, trying to place the blame for his own action upon anyone but himself. However, his hanging head and sagging shoulders demonstrated how heavy his guilt hung upon him.

Turning to the woman, who to this time had stood speechless, her shoulders also sagging as she knew the truth of all that was said, God asked, "What is this that you have done?"

"The serpent tricked me and lied to me. I too, did eat, and I gave some to Adam, my God."

Gazing intently at the serpent, who had remained so Satan could see what God's reaction would be, God began to pass judgment.

"You shall be cursed above all other animals for yielding yourself so readily to Satan. You shall crawl upon your belly with the dust of the trail in your mouth. You will strike at man's heel, and the seed of the woman shall crush your head."

Instantly, the beautiful reptile became wingless and legless. Almost, as it were, in its place there was a large King Cobra with spread hood. It dropped to the ground and crawled into the grass so Satan could listen to the rest of the proceedings.

Now, fixing His attention upon the woman, God continued, "Your sin is more grievous than Adam's, so you will always be subservient unto him. Childbirth will be painful; however, it will be as wife and mother that you shall keep your soul. Even then, your children will inherit death from you."

Lastly, He came to Adam. "Because you listened to the woman, I have cursed the land for your sake. It won't produce as well as before. It will grow thorns and thistles in abundance. By the sweat of your brow, you and your family will eat your food. You will no longer be able to live in the garden. Since you sinned willfully, and with your full knowledge, your sons and daughters will inherit their sinfulness from you. Your sinfulness will be passed on by your children."

Continuing on in another vein, God stated, "Fig Leaves will not do for a covering. Your own works will cover neither your nakedness nor your sin. Innocent blood must be shed."

Before their horrified eyes, God then killed an animal who was guilty of neither sin nor error and used its skin for clothing for them. Now the animals would die just as the preadamic ones did.

With heavy heart, God began to explain death. "You have even now, died spiritually. Your offspring also have inherited your sinfulness, so all of you will die someday."

"Oh God, is there no place of repentance for us? If death is all we have to look forward to, would it not have been more merciful to just have killed us now?" cried Adam.

God was touched by the agony in Adam's heart. "There will be a resurrection of the dead. If you follow My instructions, you will yet live when sin has been put down forever. Of Eve's seed will be born the Messiah who will save His people from their sins. He will be, in a sense, the last Adam. Where you, Adam, chose to sin, He will choose not to."

God then instructed them how to sacrifice. The animal always had to be a clean, innocent, perfect victim. It had to be offered on an altar untouched by iron tools. Also, God instructed them in the art of survival, especially, agriculture. In short, that which had not been necessary until after they sinned.

Satan was already planning on how he could get them to the tree of life. If only they could eat of that tree, they would live forever in their sinful flesh, just as they were. God would be made out a liar and be defeated.

God, however, was way out ahead of him. Michael had Heaven's version of the Green Berets standing at parade rest. They were ready to move at God's command to protect the gate to the garden. God commanded, "Secure the Garden!" Instantly, it was done. In front of the gate into Eden, a flaming atomic sword, resembling for all the world, some science fiction type cannon, sat turning in all directions. It was manned by the mighty cherubim.

No ordinary warrior angels these, they were the warrior cherubim, armed with their atomic sidearms. No mortal on Earth stood chance one against these mighty warriors even without their flaming weapons. With their weapons, no army that ever marched, human or angel, could hope to compare. When they struck, the Bible would describe it as 'fire and brimstone'.

Their tour of duty would be a short one, for God would cause the sands of the Middle East to rapidly overrun Eden. The tree of life would soon bloom only in Heaven.

Satan slunk back to his troops. Fury gave him an even more evil visage than normal. Yes, man had fallen, but he would not live forever in this state, and God had said he would be saved!

Adam and Eve were not long in comprehending just what they had given up. —oh those thorns! Adam could not always keep up with his work, and Eve would be called upon to not only do hers, but help Adam as well.

One evening, while sitting by the fire, Eve whispered to Adam as though sharing a secret, "Adam, I think I'm going to have a baby."

Adam let out a whoop and hugged her fiercely.

"Careful, my love, we don't want it to come to soon."

Adam tried, as best he could, to spare her as much work as possible until the child came.

At last, the day came, and the child, a lusty boy, was born. He made his debut whooping, and hollering, and worrying his parents no end. They had never seen a baby before. How were they to know he would be born crying?

Finally, he was quiet as he snuggled to Eve's breast. She gurgled, "I have gotten the man from God. I have given birth to the Messiah!"

No Eve. Sorry, but you are some forty odd generations ahead of schedule!

When Man Slew God

Part Two

CHAPTER XII

THE LAST WEEK

Polished masonry! Gleaming gold! Breathtaking! Thirteen men emerged from Herod's Temple, which stood gleaming in all the beauty and splendor that power and a limitless supply of money could bestow upon it. Curtains, literally a giant tapestry, four inches thick, eighty feet high, and covered by a panorama of the entire heavens, caused the humble fishermen's hearts to beat faster with pride.

"Master, did You ever see such huge and beautiful stones?"

"Yes, and look at how tight the joints are. With the gold overlay, you can hardly see them."

A pleasant looking Fellow who would have stood close to six feet tall, obediently observed each item they pointed out. A rather pained expression came over His face as He began to speak.

"See all these things, My friends? Well, look closely, for the time is coming, and isn't far off, when there won't be one stone left upon another!"

Later, as they were lounging around on the Mount of Olives, the disciples brought up the topic again. "Master, what is the sign for us to look for so we can know when to expect Your kingdom and the end of the age to take place?"

"Don't let anyone fool you. Many are going to try to, especially at the very end of the age," Jesus said.

Feeling caused His eyes to tighten and His lips to thin.

"They are going to say, 'Hey, I'm Christ,' or 'I'm going to take you to Him,' or even, 'I'm some kind of Messiah'. When this happens, just rejoice, for I will be coming soon! When I do, there won't be any doubt in anyone's mind. Every eye will see Me, no matter where you are or what you are doing. I will change you physically, and all will be caught up to meet Me if they have accepted Me as Savior."

After a pause, He continued, "There are also going to be wars and rumors of war. Don't let this frighten you either. These things have to happen, but the end won't come immediately.

"Then,[11] will come a very important sign; nation shall rise against nation, and kingdom against kingdom in a progressive escalation.

"There will be great earthquakes, people starving, epidemics, and frightening sights that would have been beyond man's wildest imagination just a short while before.

"Also, great things will begin to take place in the heavens. This is the beginning of sorrows. Like the first pains of a woman in labor, these are the first signs of the end.

"Nations are going to be in distress. They will be perplexed at the way things are going. Men are going to be so afraid that they will actually die of heart attacks because of the constant stress.

"Watch the Fig tree[12]. When its branches begin to bud[13], know that summer is getting close[14].

"Now listen closely, you guys, the generation that sees the budding of the Fig Tree won't end before I will come again for you!

"Another sign is this, when you have preached the gospel to every nation on Earth, the end will come.

"There is going to be a terrible tribulation such as has never been seen on Earth. After that, the sun will nova, even causing the moon to be darkened, and the stars will be shaken out of their orbits. This is when I will actually set foot on Earth."

The Savior's eyes narrowed as though looking deep into

the future. What He saw seemed to nearly bring physical pain.

After a thoughtful pause, He began again, "The evilness of that day will be every bit as bad as it was in the days of Noah. There will be every known excess: eating, drinking, drugs, sexual perversions. Divorce will be an everyday thing—when they even bother to marry.

"Noah was lifted above the judgment, and the wicked left. That is going to be the way it will be when I come back for you. Two will be in the field. One will be taken and the other left.

"Watch and be ready, for you sure don't want to be one of the ones left. The ones taken will be highly rewarded; however, those left have nothing but weeping and gnashing of their teeth to look forward to."

"Michael approached at a run. "Father! Satan has replaced the regular demon that he calls Ug, and who has been assigned to Jesus all of His life, and he replaced him with Rege! What would be important enough to replace a demon with a fallen angel?"

"Hum-m, with DA for a guardian angel, I'm not worried," said the Father. "If DA could defeat, bind, and escort Apollyon right through Hades and lock him in Tartarus, he should be able to handle Rege."

"Oh, I have no doubts that DA can handle any angel, other than Satan. However, Rege will be too smart to fight with DA. Caleb threw enough of a scare into him when they attacked Heaven that he is pretty careful how he puts his body in harms way, anymore. I really believe he is a more dangerous angel than Apollyon. He's nearly as vicious, nearly as tough in combat—and really smart! If Apollyon had of been as smart as he thought he was, he would never have let his viciousness get out of hand to the point that he had to be removed from Earth. You would never see Rege doing something like that."

"All right, Michael, take twelve legions of warrior angels; leave just the temple guards. You can also have the Charioteers, and the Warrior Cherubim. You will be at Battle Stations.

"You will do nothing unless Satan gets out of his bounds, or Jesus gives you orders. See that Satan knows you are there, and I'm sure he won't do anything he isn't authorized to."

Beelzebub looked up and his heart nearly froze within him. His terror-stricken eyes beheld what could literally be termed a "flying phalanx" of Heaven's angels approaching.

Pale and trembling, he staggered up to Satan. His fright caused him to forget himself enough, to paw at him.

The Devil knocked him away in his disgust. "What's the matter with you? Get yourself together!"

"B-but Master! Heaven's angels are down here!"

"Aw, knock it off!" Satan said. "It wouldn't be that bad if they were all down here. There have been guardian angels ever since the creation."

Beelzebub swallowed hard, and seemed to speak around a large lump in his throat. "They are, all down here, Master, at least all the warrior ones are."

Now, Satan paled somewhat. "You're sure?"

"Yes, Master!" Beelzebub said, misery distorting his pinched, evil little features even more than usual.

Satan was quiet for a while as he thought this out. At last he seemed to snap out of it. "Well, Jesus is expecting to die, so I have the leeway to bring about His death, anyway."

Gold, plush cushions protecting soft, fat bottoms, exotic hand carved wood. Yes, we are looking at the carved furniture of Caiaphas's gilded office. The men wore the best clothing money could buy. Their hands didn't look as though they had ever done an honest day's work. Their beards were neatly trimmed and groomed against a background of sickly white skin that obviously wasn't used to the light of the sun without some sort of protection.

Caiaphas eased his bulk into the chair, and his bottom

hung out on both sides of the cushion. His midriff roll spilled over the elaborate arm rests.

He really didn't like some of these men, for he was a Sadducee. His audience was about evenly divided between his men and the Pharisees.

As High Priest, he outranked them all; however, only in extreme circumstances would they all have gotten together—rank or no rank.

A nervous twitch of his face revealed his emotion. Sadducees didn't believe in the resurrection of the dead. Now he was told that the upstart of a Carpenter had just raised some nobody called Lazarus after he had been dead for four days. It left him looking pretty stupid.

The Pharisees gave lip service, at least, to the resurrection, but he was going to need all the help he could get if he was going to bring his plan to completion. He had to get along with them. He was also, going to have to be discreet.

"You all know that Jesus of Nazareth is the purpose of our being here," he said. "We also know that He is performing a lot of miracles. If you have been listening to His teachings, you know that if you accept what He is saying, we are out of work. We'll have to give up our power and wealth. If you accept Him as Messiah, the Romans will come and kill us all. You can see He isn't a fighting man. What chance would we stand? No, I believe it is to the advantage of our nation for Him to die for the people."

The meeting lasted about a half hour, and for once the two factions seemed to be in agreement. He had chosen his allies well. "From now on, we must set out to capture Jesus at all costs," he said with emotion, one hand clenched into a fist for emphasis.

"During the feast?" queried a pinched faced Pharisee.

"No, He's got too many followers. We'd probably get stoned. If we just had a traitor in His camp, we might accomplish it. But without, we'll just have to wait for the right opportunity that may arise."

Dandy, now a demon since being beheaded by Caleb, had

been hovering overhead with a half a dozen more disembodied spirits listening to the proceedings. He had been temporarily relieved of his duties of possessing his favorite Pharisee to take part in this important meeting. Now, he made right for Satan. As soon as he reported, Satan turned to Beelzebub. "Is there anyone close to Him who might have a weakness that we could exploit?"

Beelzebub grinned evilly, "Yah, one of His disciples. He's a guy named Judas Iscariot. He figured Jesus was going to be some sort of king, and followed Him to get on the bandwagon. He's getting pretty discouraged."

"OK, put Ug and two or three of our best demons on him. If they can't possess him, demonize him—control him."

Judas wasn't hard to find. Jesus had sent him to give some money to the poor, so they too, could enjoy the feast. This was absurd to a man such as Judas. There were so many of the poor that what they gave was only a drop in the bucket. What was worse, they didn't have much to start with. And now, they would just barely get through the feast solvent. He had only given half of what Jesus told him to, and pocketed the rest; but at this rate, he would still die in poverty when he was old.

The pouting disciple walked along, kicking the dirt like an unhappy child. If it hadn't been so unmanly, he might even have shed a tear of frustration.

"There's our man," chuckled Beelzebub, "and he looks ready to fry."

Ug and the three Cro-Magnon spirits went right to work. Judas resisted their attempts to possess him, so they concentrated on controlling his mind.

One of the spirits whispered, "Boy, for two mites, I'd break clean with this Guy. I only wish there was some way to make some cash out of this to make up for the time I've wasted." And Judus didn't even realize that it wasn't his own thought.

The demons didn't want to overdo it, and let it coast at that. From now on, however, most of Judas's thoughts would only partially be his own, if that much. The demons were in full control.

Some of Caiaphas's domestic help were followers of Jesus, and it didn't take long for word of the meeting and its outcome to get to Him.

With a slight frown turning the corners of Jesus' lips down, He asked, "What do you think, guys?"

Without waiting for anyone else to speak, Peter said, "I think it is time to get out of here!"

"Yes, Master," John agreed, "I really think You may be in more danger than usual."

Nodding thoughtfully, Jesus answered, "Yes, I think we'll head on down to Ephraim. It's just a little town, and it's pretty out of the way. When it comes the right time, I'm willing to die, but it isn't time yet."

As the feast drew nearer, however, He began to become more and more restless. Finally He said, "Well fellas, dangerous or not, it is time to return to Jerusalem."

On the other hand, Jesus wasn't a bit more restless than many of the rest of the people. Annas, Caiaphas's evil old father-in-law and co-high priest, was really pushing him. Yes, and the demons were pushing both of them. Satan was becoming impatient!

Annas glowered at his son-in-law, "Man, if you don't get on with it, feast or no feast, we are all going to be in big trouble! Can't you see we are losing? The whole world is going after this Guy! They say that Lazarus jerk came out of that tomb feet first, not even touching the ground when He raised him. And you know those grave clothes, soaked in a hundred pounds of spices, would cause him to be immobile. That's the only way he could have come out!

"Yah, and if that isn't bad enough, He's made a king's entry into Jerusalem. The whole city was out to greet Him. They tell me even the Greeks have come to question Him about His doctrine. Now, if you were made king, and had enemies like us around, what would you do?"

A harried Caiaphas stroked a paler than usual brow and

replied, "I'd nail them all to crosses, but, my friend, you don't know just how tricky it is to get hold of Him! What appear to be sure fire plans, just fall apart when we try to take Him!"

Annas stared him in the eye earnestly and replied, "Well, just figure out who you want nailed to that cross. It's either us or Him!"

So saying, Annas stood up and strode out, leaving Caiaphas mopping cold sweat from his face.

Caiaphas paced back and forth for a while, muttering to himself. "Raise Lazarus from the dead, will He? A man should kill that guy over again!"

As this thought struck him, he stopped dead in his tracks. "Hey! That isn't too bad an idea!" he shouted. "It might even smoke Jesus out!"

A startled young priest popped in with a frightened look on his face. "Did you call, Master?" he queried.

"Huh?" Caiaphas answered absent mindedly. "Oh yah, spread the word to the heads of
the Sadducees and Pharisees to stop in and see me. Just their leaders are all that will be necessary."

"Yes Sir," the priest answered, backing out quickly.

The young man moved swiftly, and within the hour, a half dozen men who would have made "Who's who" amongst the Scribes, Pharisees, and Sadducees were gathered.

Caiaphas spoke excitedly and heatedly to them. "OK, we go carefully, but rush it as much as possible. We arrest Lazarus as an enemy of the Roman Empire. When Jesus tries to defend him, we've got Him on the same charge!"

Pinched Face Pharisee added, "Really, Jesus is who we are after. If we capture Him before we get Lazarus, we can forget him. He's just small fry, right?"

"Right," responded Caiaphas.

Caiaphas would have hugged himself had he known that at that very moment, Jesus and His disciples were nearing Bethany. Shortly, both they and Lazarus, with Mary and Martha, would be dining in the home of Simon the Leper. Caiaphas didn't know; however, and God would give these beloved followers this supper almost unblemished.

The only mar would probably save Lazarus's life. His death would now, be unnecessary. All were through eating, and were visiting and worshipping God. Mary walked around behind Jesus, and with about as much regard for the beautiful alabaster box as she would have had for an egg shell, she smashed it, and poured the pure spikenard over Jesus's head.

"Would you look at that idiocy?" a demon fairly screamed into Judas's mind; and Judas blew his top. Evilness can be infectious, and he carried some of the rest along with him, momentarily.

"This stupid wench!" he raved. "This is the second time she has pulled something like this![15] She's wasted two full years income for the average man now. Just think what that could have done for the poor!"

"Yah, and you'd probably have managed to skim at least a fourth of it!" a demon reminded him.

Instantly, Jesus came to her rescue. "Hey! Leave her alone! She's done a very fine thing. In fact, wherever the gospel is preached, this will be told as a memorial to her. You will always have the poor with you, but you won't always have Me. What she has done is anoint My body for burial."

Judas spun on his heel and headed for the door. This reaction wasn't exactly unusual for him. Since he was the treasurer who ran errands, he came and went a good deal. The disciples didn't think much of it. There was a sad look in Jesus's eyes; however, as He watched him go. He knew precisely what was going on in his mind.

Judas's mind was, indeed, in a turmoil. As Beelzebub had said, he had joined Jesus's party initially, because he thought Jesus would become king of liberated Israel. It only made sense to him to get in on the ground floor with the new monarch. This way should lead to luxury.

Things hadn't gone as he had expected, and he had gotten only that which he could skim off the money bag, which was entrusted to him.

Now, Jesus was talking of dying. If this was a sinking ship, Judas was getting off! He had wasted over three years of his life, and he was going to get something out of it. If

Jesus was so bent on dying, he would just help Him along a bit. He would sell Him to the Chief Priest!

When Judas, since he was a disciple of Jesus, showed up asking for Caiaphas, he was ushered right in.

The old villain looked up at him with distrust common to all such men who are steeped in ungodliness. "What business does a disciple of the Carpenter have with me?" he asked.

Judas grinned smugly, and answered his question with one of his own. "What will you give me for Jesus?"

Not to be taken lightly, and still suspicious, Caiaphas sneered, "Oh, I suppose you have Him right there in your pouch?"

Judas still wasn't in any mood to be trifled with. His smile died instantly. He had just walked out of one door, and two wouldn't make his day any worse.

He started to turn to leave, and Caiaphas realized his error. He motioned to a large servant who was dressed as a scribe, and who looked as though he might be more useful for his brawn than his ability to write.

The fellow reached out, and caught Judas from behind by the arms between the biceps and elbow. Holding them in against Judas's body, he lifted him off the floor. After a pause for effect, he set him back where he had been. The strength and the grip put just enough fear in Judas that he was glad to see that now, Caiaphas was smiling at him.

"Take it easy, my firebrand," he soothed. "Don't I have the right to be a little cautious? Now, tell me how you are going to sell me Jesus, when I can't even find Him."

Judas became serious and businesslike now. "Without help, you'll never take Him. He has so many friends to help Him that He can slip in and out of the city, and you'll never be the wiser. That's where I come in. I'll take you to Him the first time He is in town—ah-h-h, shall we say, for a fee?"

Caiaphas again, became cautious, "What sort of fee?"

Between Bethany and Jerusalem, Judas had gotten that pretty well figured out too. "The price of a good male slave, thirty pieces of silver," he answered without hesitation.

Caiaphas's first impulse was to dicker. However, the expression on Judas's face and the memory of how quickly he had started to just leave when crossed before, removed the inclination. "And if I go along, how are we going to get together?"

"I know Him very well," returned Judas, "and since I'm His business manager, I pretty well come and go without question. I'll just come and get you."

A funny little smile crossed Caiaphas's face. "You're His business manager? I suppose He would use wolves to guard his sheep too?"

Even Judas had to smile a little at that.

"Is He going to be in town for the feast?" asked Caiaphas.

"Oh no!" parried Judas. "Thirty pieces of silver, and when He does come, I'll turn Him over to you, but that is all the information you get from me!"

"All right," Caiaphas replied. "And to show you that I trust you, we'll pay you right now. Of course, you realize that if you don't come through, that makes you a thief—and thieves get nailed to crosses! I'm sure you'll be a very honest man!"

Judas headed back for Bethany, his pouch heavy with the silver coins. At times, his conscience would prick him a little; however, the thought of hanging on a cross didn't appeal to him at all. He couldn't help having a certain amount of admiration for the old fox of a priest. He might have lost his nerve and backed out on the whole thing, otherwise. But that cross in the background really ruled that out!

CHAPTER XIII

THE LAST SUPPER

Crowds naturally gathered around Jesus, even when He was travelling. Thus, one wouldn't even have known that He was arriving in Jerusalem if one had looked at the people jamming the road during this holiday.

Christ walked along with Peter and John on each side of Him. As they entered the gate,

He commanded, "Peter, you and John go make arrangements for preparing the Passover Supper for us."

Peter replied, "Lord, where and how do we prepare this supper? There is nothing to eat and nowhere to cook it if there was."

"Peter, have I ever sent you to do something that you couldn't do?" answered Jesus. "When you get into the city, you'll meet a man carrying a pitcher of water. Follow him home, and ask him where the guest room is so I can eat the Passover with My disciples. He'll show it to you."

Peter didn't have nerve enough to ask about the food. Probably, if finding somewhere to cook it was that easy, the food would take care of itself too.

Christ and the rest of the disciples stayed on the outskirts of town until the other two got back.

The two friends were strolling along, and true to form, Peter was fretting, "John! I hate this kind of thing! Do you suppose we will really meet this guy with a pitcher?"

John smothered a grin at the big burly Peter. "Sure we will. Jesus said we would, didn't He?"

"Yah," Peter responded, "What I mean is, I sure hope it's the right guy with a pitcher, so he will let us have the room."

"Aw, quit your fretting, Pal, Jesus won't let us down."

Before Peter could respond, they looked up and saw a fellow approaching with a pitcher of water. John nudged Peter, and put his finger to his lips. Normally, only women did this chore, so this just about had to be their man. They let the guy go past, and then fell in behind him at a discreet distance.

In spite of his tendency to be a 'Luie the Lip', this wasn't to Peter's liking. Using a stage whisper that could be heard ten feet away, he whispered into John's ear, "You do the talking!"

John might not stand out like big bold Peter, but well did Jesus nickname he and his brother James, 'The Sons of Thunder'.

"That's all right," John replied. "Just leave it to me."

The man seemed to be nearing his home, and John picked up the pace. Just before he entered the door, John spoke—
"Sir—"

The man looked around in surprise. Recognition crossed his features. "Oh, you're Jesus's disciples. What can I do for you?"

"Ah—'er" without thinking, Peter began to stutter, but John cut in, "Sir, Jesus needs somewhere to eat supper with His disciples. Can you help us?"

"Sure. I've got a large upper room—all furnished. Be my guest."

After he had shown them the room, they returned to Christ. "All right, Judas, Now you can go to the meat market and buy a lamb for supper."

"If there is enough money to buy a lamb," he thought.

To the continuing surprise of all, there was just enough money in the poke to buy what they needed.

Now the rest could come into town and relax as well as help with the meal.

As many enemies as Jesus had, it wouldn't do for Him to be seen running around in broad daylight. He had prayed earnestly to the Father for the chance to eat this supper with His disciples. Even the Son of God would not tempt the Father.

The large upper room made a very comfortable place for them to lounge in. They visited with trusted friends and relatives, and smelled the delightful aromas coming from the cooking food.

Judas thought about going to the Chief Priest then, but decided to put it off for a while. In spite of his evil nature, he hated to do it; and too, there was a terrific meal coming up. Why spoil that?

Later that evening, when it was only Jesus and His disciples, Jesus sat down and began to speak. There was a slight catch in His throat as He said, "I have really wanted to have the opportunity to eat this meal with you before I suffer. I won't get to eat it again until we eat it fresh in the Kingdom of Heaven."

Reaching over and picking up a loaf of bread, He blessed it, broke it into pieces, and passed it around saying, "Here, take this bread and eat it. This is My body which is broken for you. Do this every so often in remembrance of Me." Then lifting the large communal container of wine, He said, "You must also drink some of this, for it is My blood which is shed for the sins of all who will accept Me."

Changing the subject, Jesus turned to Peter and said, "Simon, Satan would dearly love to just sift you like wheat; however, I have prayed for you that your faith doesn't fail."

Peter swelled up in indignation and replied, "Fail? Me? Man, you gotta be kiddin'! I don't care if it means prison or death, You'll find old Peter right there along side You!"

Jesus grinned and shook His head, "Peter, before the second crowing of the cock, you'll deny Me three times!"

Before Peter could object anymore, Christ arose and laid aside His outer garments. He, then, wrapped a towel around Himself. Someone should have washed their feet after walking barefoot or in sandals on the dusty roads. Everyone had waited, hoping to outfumble the rest—now here was Jesus doing it. Everyone felt like they could walk through the door without opening it—under it! —with it closed—without even having to duck their heads!

Jesus poured water into a basin, and proceeded to wash their feet with the disciples sitting there nearly speechless. When He approached Peter, poor old Peter again, had to put mouth in motion before putting brain in gear. "Lord, would you actually wash my feet? Oh no! I'm not about to let you degrade Yourself that much!"

Jesus shook His head resignedly. "Peter, if you don't let Me wash your feet, you have just cut yourself completely out of having any part with Me."

In a reaction typical of Peter, he answered, "Lord, if it's that important, give me a bath!"

The Lord chuckled at the big lovable fisherman. "My friend, if you have been bathed, all you need thereafter is to wash your hands and feet. Your feet are what's dirty in this case. Later on, after you have been converted, your daily sins will have to be cleansed as you go along."

Speaking to everyone now, He continued, "This is an example of humbleness and humility. Where I have done this for you, the least you can do is do it for one another. Bear one another's burdens and uphold them in moments of weakness."

The newly instituted ceremony completed, they settled down to eating in earnest. With the edge off their appetites, Jesus raised His head and spoke. "You know something fellows? The guy who will betray Me is sitting right here at the table with us!"

Judas's stomach tied up in knots, and his hair stood on end. How could this Guy know all these things? If He knew that much, He also knew who it was. All He would have to do would be speak his name for the other eleven to beat him to death!

Jesus continued, "Sure, this is the way it was meant to be, but woe be it to the man by whom I am betrayed!"

The rest of the disciples didn't actually understand what

He meant. They even wondered if something they had done had caused His betrayal.

"Lord, is it I? Is it I?" they asked.

Judas had been very quiet with his head down. Suddenly, he realized that this made him more conspicuous than if he acted like the rest. With an air of nonchalance, he dipped his bread into the dish right along side of Christ and asked, "Is it I?"

Jesus answered, "The guy with his hand in the dish with Me!"

Judas was terror stricken. However, Jesus's answer, phrased as it was, probably saved his life; for the rest didn't catch the significance of the remark.

Judas's heart almost stopped within him for a moment until he realized this. As frightened as he was, he was about to decide that selling Jesus was simply too risky. Then Jesus dipped a piece of bread in the gravy and handed it to him. Instantly, he was demon possessed. No, not by Ug, Dandy, or some such, by Satan, himself. Then as many others as he might need began moving in as Satan held the door wide for them!

Immediately, his fear subsided. The demons knew they had better not goof up now. The boss was riding along. They knew Satan had to have this man. They didn't often soothe anyone, but this was an exception.

"Get it over with, fella," Jesus ordered, not unkindly, and Judas left. The others supposed that he had been sent off on some errand.

After Judas left, Jesus turned to the rest and asked, "When I sent you out without purse, bag, nor sandals, did you lack anything?"

"Nothing," they replied.

"All right," He continued, "from now on, you will take both purse and bag as well as swords. From now on, poverty will be no asset.[16]"

"Swords?" queried Peter in surprise.

"Yes, it is written that I will be numbered with the transgressors. You have to look the part."

After one of the disciples produced a short sword, Peter, with the look of a child caught with his hand in the cooky jar, pulled one from his robe that was full grown. Trying to look nonchalant and innocent, he remarked, "This makes two."

With a bemused look on His face, Christ returned, "That will do quite well."

"O.K., fellas," He continued, "let's sing a hymn and go to the Garden of Gethsemane."

As the disciples were leaving, Judas entered the high-ceilinged office of Caiaphas.

"Ah, I had begun to wonder if you had forgotten," crooned the fat old slob. "Have you got Him for us?"

Now all fear was gone, and Judas felt really important. "I can take you to Him," he said, strutting back and forth. "It could be fairly dark, according to where He is when we find Him; so I will kiss Him on the cheek. From that, your men will know they have the right man. He may not be where I left Him, but never fear, I can find Him!"

"It will take a while to get our men together," Caiaphas replied, "so just wait here for a time."

The disciples felt a little better since it was dark. At least, it would be harder to recognize them. The moon was shining; however, this merely gave them a little light to see by.

Jesus didn't seem the least bit apprehensive. He did seem somewhat depressed, which was unusual for Him. About half way across the bridge which spanned the brook Cedron, He stopped and gazed absently at the reflection of the moon in the crystal water below. He took a deep breath, enjoying the smell of flowers and blooming trees. A slight breeze brought the scent of the city to Him, and he didn't even find this offensive.

His elbow rested on the rail and His chin on His hand. He really didn't seem to be in a hurry to do anything. In fact, He seemed to be savoring every sight and sound as they walked along.

At last, they entered the Garden of Gethsemane. Jesus

left the main body of the disciples, and taking Peter, James, and John, went on about thirty yards, stopped, and began to pray.

The import of what was about to happen started to bear down on Him now, and He began to take an emotional beating.

Realizing that this was a bit too traumatic for the three men, He left them and went on a ways farther and got down to some very deep praying.

Here, the human side of Jesus started to make itself felt. He knew exactly what was going to happen to Him, and it almost frightened Him to death.

Since Jesus's human side was in control of His emotions now, He was vulnerable. Rege seized the moment, and moved in to badger Him. No way was he going to leave this to a demon, or for that matter, any number of demons. Failure here would mean facing Satan—no thanks!

Meanwhile, Satan, having turned Judas over to Ug and company, got together with sharp witted little Beelzebub and discussed the problem on both their minds. "Why would God allow us to kill Jesus?" worried Satan. "What are we missing?"

"Could it be the method by which He dies?" asked Beelzebub. "Crucifixion seems to be the only permissible way."

"Possibly, but even with crucifixion, the Kingdom of Heaven is finished if Jesus dies," Satan returned thoughtfully. "Since He is sinless, Jesus can live and reign forever as Israel's Messiah, Priest, and King. Why would He allow us to kill him by any method?"

"Perhaps we are making a mistake by going along with them and killing Him," suggested Beelzebub.

Satan looked at him contemptuously. "Sure, then the Kingdom of Heaven will be set up immediately; no, we have to kill Him. We just don't dare make any mistakes while we're at it."

"All right, we have determined that He has to die despite whatever consequences there are—even if that means a cross; which seems to be God's plan. What if we kill Him some other way?"

"Those twelve legions of angels would attack immediately," Satan returned in disgust.

"No, I mean kill Him by such means as a heart attack brought on by fear. Maybe induce the humans to kill Him some other way. The instant reality deviates from God's plan, we've won; haven't we?"

Satan sat, nodding thoughtfully as he thrashed out in his mind, all the effects and countereffects that he could think of.

"The demons say Jesus is concentrating on His earthly problems to such an extent that perhaps for the first time since He was born, He might be vulnerable," continued Beelzebub.

"As far as His body is concerned, He is human. He is God in a human body. I can't believe He'd leave Himself that vulnerable, He didn't do that when He was Melchisedec," agreed Satan, still deep in thought. Coming to a decision, he continued, "Take word to Rege. Bear down on Jesus hard enough to cause Him to die of a heart attack or something. Then, if that doesn't work, influence the soldiers or the crowd to kill Him. As a last resort, He dies on a cross. And if that happens, EVERYONE! Everyone will answer to me!"

Satan reached out and gripped Beelzebub's arm for a moment to keep him from leaving while he continued to think. "Tell Rege to keep on trying to get Him to quit for a while, before he tries to get Him killed. He seems just a little to ready to die for my liking. For some reason that I don't understand, He seems to have to die for man to be saved. I also, don't know how this ties into His Kingdom on Earth, but we have to stop that. If we can make God alter His plan in any way, we've won."

Beelzebub fairly sprinted to Rege; and as he approached, DA knew a moment of apprehension. The odds didn't look too good.

One of the righteous spirits raced to Michael. "Michael! Beelzebub has joined Rege!"

Michael looked pained. "Oh, if I just weren't too busy to personally go help him!"

Michael looked around at the troops, and a good-looking blond angel stepped up. "Sir, may I go?"

Michael was pleased. This guy was tough in a smooth, scientific, almost sanitary way. He was the kind who probably wouldn't even have any dust on his robe afterward if it did come to a fight. He would, however, be on top. It wouldn't do for Rege to underestimate Raphael.

Even as Michael debated what to do, Big Caleb shuffled his feet and looked miserable.

Michael sighed his relief as he said, "All right, Raphael. Move! Quickly! —and yes, Caleb, you can go too!"

"Pie Yeminny, I thank ye, Sar—"

"Caleb! Shut up and get!" Michael ordered.

Death Angel was prepared for battle. He had no idea what the two satanic angels were going to do. If they thought they were going to do any personal damage to Jesus, they better think again. By the time they had come over the top of him, they would know they had been in a fight.

DA was concentrating on the action in front of him. When a hand came to rest on his shoulder, the muscles tightened into ropes, and he flinched.

"Sorry, DA. I didn't mean to frighten you. I thought you might like a little help. If nothing else, we can lend you moral support."

"Oh, Hello, Raphael. It's worth a little scare to have you and Caleb around."

Raphael and DA were a contrast in opposites. Even though both were big and good-looking, they were big and good-looking in different ways. Raphael was blonde and smooth featured—perhaps fine featured. There was, however, nothing weak about him. DA, on the other hand, was dark complexioned with black hair. His features were heavy while being smooth and nearly handsome. They were heightened by his battle scars. Caleb was the picture of masculinity. You couldn't really say the big redhead was handsome, but a woman wouldn't have found him repulsive either. Yes, and he was big! He stood a head taller than either of the other two angels, as big as they were.

On the other side, Rege towered above the scrubby Beelzebub. He too, was dark, even darker than DA. Beelzebub's complexion, on the other hand, was mottled, his hair the color of dirty, weathered straw. Rege was handsome in a fine, weak way. His eyes were black and evil, possibly a little small and a bit too close together. His nose was straight and almost sharp enough to cut with. It was set off by a pencil line mustache. He also wore a pointed, black Vandyke goatee; which, he wore to look as much as possible like Satan, who also wore them. While not as smart as Beelzebub, he was evilness personified.

With a big grin, which was trying to escape the underbrush of his huge red handlebar mustache, Caleb waved to Rege. "Aye, do ye remember me, lad?"

The fact that he studiously ignored him showed that, indeed, Rege did remember the mighty Caleb.

The invisible Rege approached Jesus, and an equally invisible DA cut him off. "What do you think you're going to do?" demanded DA.

"I'm not going to touch Him, and you have no right to stop me from doing anything else I wish to do," sneered the evil angel.

"Maybe not, but you step over the line in any way, and you'll be dead and in Tartarus without even knowing how you got there! You won't even get to hang around as a disembodied spirit!"

Rege simply tossed his head disdainfully, and stepped around DA. He sat down beside the praying Jesus, and began to speak directly to His mind.

"Look, Pal, You don't have to go through with this. God must have some kind of backup plan. Anyway, that rough old splintery cross isn't going to be exactly comfortable. Did You ever stop to think about what it is going to feel like when a big, tough Roman soldier pounds a rough, rusty square spike through Your hands and feet? Oh yah, and he will do it slowly so it'll hurt as badly as possible?

"Also, wouldn't it be neat to go ahead and live out Your life time here on Earth—live here forever, for that matter. You haven't sinned. You don't have to die. Maybe You could have one of those good looking women that have been ministering to Your needs for a wife? How about Mary Magdalene? She's neat. Maybe You could raise some kids? Like a boy to carry on Your name?"

DA stepped in and said, "Jesus—," but Jesus wasn't listening.

Jesus had never quit praying, and now He continued, "Father, all things are possible with You. I know that You can arrange it so I don't have to go through with this. Nevertheless, not My will, but Yours is what I want."

Rege cursed and kicked Beelzebub on the shin. Beelzebub whimpered, grabbed his leg and sniffled, "What'd I do? Why did ya have to do that?"

Caleb raised his hand to a little over shoulder height to get their attention and asked, "Aye, lads, would ye let me do that fer ya?"

After praying for a while in this vain, and with His heart nearly breaking, Jesus thought of His disciples. Wondering how they were taking it all, He went back to see how they were doing. To His surprise, He found them sleeping. His concern turned to indignation. At the worst moment of His life, they were asleep!

"Peter! Couldn't you even watch and pray with Me for an hour or so? Man, you better stay prayed up! I know your spirit is willing, but the flesh is weak! Keep praying or you will fall into temptation!"

Seeing that the rest were all right, He went back and resumed His praying. Never had He prayed with such fervor and so little success. For one thing, as much as He wanted out of this, He knew that He was praying in His own will and not the Father's. For the first and only time in His life, He didn't have faith that God would answer His prayer.

This time, Rege and Beelzebub weren't trying to talk Jesus out of dying. Now they were using His own knowledge of what was to happen to Him to try to kill Him. His heart was nearly breaking, and they were trying to get it to do so—literally.

After another racking half-hour, Jesus came again to check on His disciples. He found them asleep. This time, He just shook His head and left them there.

Once again, He went back and really got down to prayer. As earnestly as He had prayed before, it was nothing compared to now. It felt as if the weight of the world was upon His shoulders. He prayed in such an agony that the small capillary veins just under the skin burst. He actually sweat blood!

Rege and Beelzebub, in spite of their distaste for each other, grabbed one another and danced an impromptu jig. When they discovered that Jesus wasn't going to die; however, all their joy fled. What was with this Guy? God would not allow His perfect sacrifice to die any way except the death for which He was born!

Again, they began upon Him. Everything on Earth that bothered Him was magnified a hundred fold. This was coupled with His natural fear of the horrible death of the cross. The human body can take only so much, and Jesus was only moments away from a heart attack when relief arrived.

Gabriel appeared in their midst and commanded, "That's it, creeps. Back up. You're all done, for now."

"You can't—you ain't got the right—"

"I can—I have—and if you want to challenge me, Michael is right behind me with the troops."

"You don't need Michael," DA said in a voice just above a whisper. "Just let us at 'em!"

The expression on the faces of the holy angels convinced the two fallen ones that discretion was a lot smarter than heroism, and they headed for Satan to report. Pride wouldn't allow them to hurry until they were out of sight, and they couldn't resist a certain amount of swagger as they walked away.

Michael arrived at this moment, and asked, "Did I miss something?"

"No," answered Gabriel. "There wasn't any fight in the cowards; and you didn't want to see what they were doing to the Lord."

Michael looked at Jesus and nodded sadly, "Well fellas, stand guard for me, will you? I've got a mission to perform, and I don't want to have to watch my back trail."

"You got it," promised Gabriel.

Just as it seemed that He would die of sorrow and fear, a man appeared by Jesus's side. At first He was startled, then knowledge dating to before He had taken human flesh caused Him to recognize the visitor.

"Michael! Fella, am I ever glad to see you!"

One thing about it, whether He went ahead and was crucified or not, it wasn't going to happen while the big warrior chieftain of the angel realm was here! If he so wished, this guy could make an endangered species out of the whole Roman Empire so quickly they wouldn't even know how it happened—and do it all by himself!

Christ had been lying against a stump, and the mighty angel sat down and cradled His head much like a parent might a child. In spite of the familiarity, there was respect in his voice when he spoke.

"Master, have You thought through what the consequences are going to be if You don't die as the plan is?"

Immediately, both the comfort of the big angel and the getting His mind off of His own problems began to be apparent. What, indeed, would be the consequence?

Michael was speaking again, "Lord, if you don't go ahead as the Lamb of God, what of Abraham, Isaac, and Jacob? Have You thought of David and Daniel? If you don't die for them, these men who have believed on You from Adam to now have believed a lie. They are lost!"

If Satan could have listened in on the conversation, doubtlessly, the crucifixion would never have taken place. He would have known the plan. But with twelve legions of Heaven's angels, the charioteers, and the warrior cherubim gathered around, no demon or fallen angel could approach close enough to hear. The words spoken were known only to those in the garden.

Jesus was rapidly beginning to get control of Himself now; however, He still had a ways to go.

Michael, the true soldier, wasn't surprised, and was ready with another wave of attack. "What of these men lying back there on the ground, Lord? Are you going to let them spend eternity in Hell?"

Jesus looked back to where the three were asleep. These men lost? —to spend eternity in Hell? Oh, what a terrible thought!

Again Michael was breaking into His thoughts, "and how about those of the future? —folks You will love as dearly as these?"

"Aw, Michael," He wailed. "I must try, but what if the flesh can't take it?"

"That is where I come in, Lord. All the warrior angels of Heaven are at Battle Stations tonight. At the least whisper of command, we will rescue You and make these rotten Romans as well as a goodly crowd of Scribes, Pharisees, and Saddusees look as though they had been trodden in the wine press!"

Suddenly, Jesus realized that He felt as though He could do it. A sense of relief and exultation flowed through Him. The Human side of His nature was conquered.

It would seem good; however, to know that Michael was ready, yes aching, later on when He was going through the man-made hell of the Crucifixion, to do just as he had promised.

In fact, Michael would forget the great advice he had just given the Lord. He would beg the Father to turn him and his mighty fighting legions loose. One thing is for sure, had God done so, during the brief period of time that they lasted, he would have made believers of all the evil men on Earth!

Meanwhile, Caiaphas had gotten a motley mob together for Judas, and they were on their way.

CHAPTER XIV

THE BEGINNING OF THE END

Focusing his gaze upon Judas with his best Dracula smile, evil old Caiaphas gurgled, "Judas, this is my most trusted servant, Malchus, I believe you met him here before. He will lead the men. All you have to do is take him to Jesus."

Looking up at the huge brute of a man, Judas stuttered something that no one understood. All Judas could think of was, "Servant nothing, more like chief high executioner!"

Caiaphas had born down a little more heavily on 'have to do' than Judas thought necessary. Really, he wasn't telling Judas anything he didn't already know!

First, Judas led the mob to the house where the supper had been eaten. They crashed the door, only to find everyone gone. A guttural, animal growl came from deep in Malchus's chest, and it stood Judas's hair on end. With dry lips, he stammered, "H-hey man, I told you they might not be here. Just hold on there. We'll find them!"

Malchus gripped his arm. Pain shot from elbow to shoulder. The huge man uttered only one word, "Fast!"

Next, Judas headed for the Mount of Olives. There was a garden there called Gethsemane, where Jesus loved to go. Judas was pretty sure that would be where they would find Him.

Meanwhile, with Michael gone and His praying finished, Jesus came back to His sleeping disciples. Looking down at them with a sigh, He whispered, as much to Himself as to them, "Sleep on, fellas, and get your rest."

Shortly thereafter, He saw the glow of the lanterns and torches, and heard the noise of the crowd. He commanded, "Rise up! My betrayer is at hand!"

The frightened disciples hit their feet, but it was too late, Judas had arrived!

Judas spoke lovingly, and stepped forward to kiss Jesus on the cheek.

Jesus sidestepped him, and asked, "Judas, would you really betray Me with a kiss?"

This was all the mighty Malchus needed. This was the man he had been sent after, and nothing would stop him.

—or would it? Eighteen hundred years or so later, men would say that all men are the same size in Judge Colt's Court; where attorneys Smith and Wesson plead their cases, and bullets cut men down to size. This was very much Peter's philosophy.

His hand was already sliding down to the hilt beneath his robe, and below that was over two feet of razor sharp, burnished steel!

Rege noticed the movement and guessed its purpose. Great! That might cause a riot in which Jesus would be killed.

"That's right, Peter! Take his head off! If you have to go, you might as well die fighting!"

DA also saw what was about to happen, and without thinking of the consequences, had to agree with Rege for once.

"You bet, Peter! Cut him down!"

Peter's gaze was riveted on Malchus's mighty bull neck, right at the base of his ear. When Peter moved, the same move that brought the sword into the light of the torches, propelled it to the spot at which he was looking.

The sword hardly caused a swish in the air as it cut a vicious arc toward the big manservant's head.

Malchus's animal like instincts were all that saved him. Out of the corner of his eye, he caught the glint of light on steel, and tipped his head. He saved his head, but not his ear. He also lost a goodly portion of the blood lust that had been driving him. "Whew! That was close!"

"Peter! Put up the sword!" cried Jesus. "The Father has poured Me this cup, and I must drink it! If I need rescuing, I have over twelve legions of angels at My command."

Malchus towered a head taller than Jesus. Jesus reached up and grasped the ear, which was dangling by a small thread of skin, and placed it back. It was healed so cleanly that you couldn't even tell it had been cut off.

Now, all were standing in awe, and Jesus asked, "Who are you seeking?"

Someone got up enough nerve to say, "Jesus of Nazareth."

"I am He," He replied.

An awful, supernatural fear gripped them, and they staggered back, falling to the ground. They would take Him, all right, but there would be no doubt in anyone's mind that He would go of His own accord. No power on Earth could overcome Him. As the humans crumpled to the ground, Beelzebub and Rege cringed in fear. It had been thousands of years since this same power had been aimed at them, but it seemed as yesterday.

Again, He asked, "Who do you seek?" and again, they answered, "Jesus of Nazareth."

"OK, I'm your man. I taught daily in your temple. Why are you coming after Me now with swords and clubs?" Without even waiting for an answer, He continued, "All right, you've got Me. I'm the one you want, so let these others go."

No one was in any mood to argue with Him in the eerie, half-light of Gethsemane. They were only too glad that He was willing to go with them quietly.

Most of the rest of the disciples turned and fled now. Peter and John, along with a few others, however, followed at a distance. One fellow, dressed in a linen sheet, got a little too close, and one of the mob tried to catch him. In his fright, he rolled out of the sheet, and ran away in his birthday suit.

Malchus took Jesus by the arm and led Him first to Annas, and then to Caiaphas, but he would never quite get over the experience in the garden. He would always hold this Man in awe.

Since Annas had seniority, even though Caiaphas was acting High Priest, Malchus had to take Christ to him first. Malchus knew Caiaphas would fret at how much time was taken, and he had little hope that Caiaphas would be understanding.

Annas looked up, saw the Lord, and roared, "This Man's a felon. Why isn't He bound?"

The soldiers jumped to comply, and roughly bound Jesus's hands behind His back. The cords cut into His flesh; however, He knew that this was nothing compared to what was coming, so He never even changed expression.

Annas raved and shouted at Christ, but got no response. Little of what he said even made sense. In his rage and frustration, he was nearly incoherent. His fat old heart fluttered a warning, and he knew a touch of fear.

After a time, he caught his breath and commanded, "Get Him out of here! Caiaphas will be waiting to question Him. Don't waste any time!"

"At least any more than we already have!" thought Malchus. However, he said not a word and his expression remained blank.

The mob was getting over their fear of Him now. In the light of the building and bound, Jesus didn't seem nearly so awesome. They shoved Him, stumbling and out of balance, into the night air, and on to Caiaphas's place.

Peter and John continued to follow along behind, and when Christ was taken into Caiaphas's, John just walked up and asked to be let in. John had known Caiaphas in the past, and was let in without question. He knew that since he was known, he couldn't hide anyway, so why fake it?

It was not so with Peter. If He could have died along side of Jesus, swinging his mighty broadsword, this he could have done with ease. But to walk into that house meekly was something else. Peter was afraid.

When it became obvious that he wasn't going to be captured and bound, John went back to the door and asked the girl who kept it to let Peter in. This she did without hesitation.

Rege was still trying his best to cause Jesus to die of fright or a broken heart. For want of anything better to do, Beelzebub chose Peter to pick on.

As Peter walked in, the girl asked, "Oh, you're also one of this Man's disciples, aren't you?"

Beelzebub tapped Peter on the shoulder, and whispered to his mind, "Hey man! If this broad finds out who you really are, she'll squeal to that fat pig of a Caiaphas, and he'll nail you to a cross right along side of yer boss!"

Peter didn't stop to think that John had been let in without being molested, and the girl knew John to be one of Jesus's disciples. He, doubtlessly, could just have said, "Sure," and that would have been all there would have been to it. However, again, Peter put mouth in motion without benefit of thought. Attempting to look nonchalant, he answered, "Me? Naw! I just stopped in to see what all the commotion was about."

Beelzebub hugged himself. One way or another, Jesus was going to be killed, and even His followers were falling apart! Satan might even give him a good word for this!

Poor old Peter couldn't win for losing. As he walked over to the fire, one of the house maids, who had seen big bold Peter somewhere else, remarked, "Say! This guy is also one of Jesus's disciples!"

A shiver ran over Peter that wasn't from the cold, and he lied, "Woman, I never met the man!"

Caiaphas glared at Jesus and asked, "How many disciples do You have, and what do you teach them?" He really wasn't genuinely interested. He only wanted something to accuse Him of and was fishing, hoping to get lucky.

Jesus answered, "Look, I spoke in every synagogue in the country, as well as the temple. I haven't said anything in secret. Ask those who have heard Me!"

An officer standing by, slapped Him an openhanded blow

that made His head snap, and said, "Is that the way You speak to the High Priest?"

After spitting blood on the beautiful tiled floor, Jesus looked the fellow in the eye and answered, "If I have said anything wrong, tell Me what it was. If not, what are you hitting me for?"

Caught for a loss of words, the soldier could only drop his head.

Caiaphas didn't like this. He had seen Jesus, with His quick wit and smooth tongue, get the upper hand on his men too many times. He wasn't about to let this happen tonight.

"Bring on the witnesses," he ordered.

He hadn't had the easiest time finding men who would be willing to testify against Jesus, and the ruffians who came in probably wouldn't have been accepted in most trials. He was desperate, however.

The first question fired at them was, "Do you recognize this Man?"

"Duh-h, yah. His name's Jesus, er somethin' like thet, ain't-ut?"

"Is it or isn't it?" roared a centurion standing by.

"Yah, that's who He is," answered one of the other witnesses.

"What has He done?" asked Caiaphas, again trying to get control of the situation.

"Oh yah, I know!" answered witness number one, trying to redeem himself. "He said He would tear the Temple down and rebuild it in a week." He smiled ingratiatingly, and showed a mouth with several missing teeth.

"No! We was supposed ta say three days," cut in witness number two—and Caiaphas blew his top.

"Get them out of here!" he shouted.

Jesus didn't even bother answering, and Caiaphas got up in stages. He uncoiled his bulk from the chair, and walked over to Jesus. Speaking as though the accusations were really serious, he demanded, "Aren't You even going to respond to these charges that have been brought against You?"

Still, Jesus refused to answer, placing Caiaphas in the same category as his hired hoods.

Caiaphas was evil to the core, but he wasn't any fool. There was one question he was sure that Jesus would answer.

"I command You in the name of the living God to speak. Are You the Son of God?"

When Jesus did speak, He didn't pull any punches. "You better believe it!" He replied. "You'll see the day when you see Me on the right hand of power, and coming in the clouds of Heaven."

This was all Caiaphas needed. He ripped the hem of his robe, as was the legal custom when one heard blasphemy. He was careful not to tear it badly enough to make it hard to mend however. With what he hoped was a fierce look, he shouted, "He has uttered blasphemy! We don't need any witnesses. You have heard Him yourselves!"

Now, setting the mood for the others, he hacked deep in his throat and spit directly in Jesus's face. That which Jesus had feared in Gethsemane had started.

A smashing blow to the side of the head all but took an ear off. Another to the face brought twin spurts of blood from His nose. A sense of exhilaration went through Him. Reality wasn't as bad as the suspense of waiting. He would be able to take it!

Someone wrapped a dirty old rag around His eyes, and tied it tightly. His head began to snap and jerk with the rain of blows as they landed solidly on a head too proud to even attempt to duck the unseen punches.

"Prophesy, if You're the Son of God. Who hit You?" they mocked. Somewhere, Satan hugged himself in glee. He hadn't been able to get Him to quit in the garden. However, with the chosen group of men, angels, and demons he had at his disposal tonight, if he didn't cause Him to break, and call upon Michael, it wouldn't be because he didn't have the right crew to do it with!

"They're going to condemn Him to death, Master," said Beelzebub when he reported to Satan.

"But I don't want Him condemned to death! I want Him

dead!" snapped Satan, who was confused enough that he really didn't know what he wanted. "Otherwise, I want Him to choose to live on out of God's will, and leave men to live on in death! —unless we can cause His death short of the cross. In fact I don't think I want Him to live under any circumstances. If He lives, he'll reign. If He does that, I've lost no matter what happens." Mellowing somewhat, he continued, "Even if Christ makes it through the torture we have in store for Him alive, I don't think that even the Son of God can stand the pain of the cross, while able to call it off at will. We must kill Him before He is nailed to that cross! Jesus's death on the cross is preferable only to His living as King! If He chooses to come down from the cross, then for sure, some way we must kill Him!"

Satan sat quietly for a few moments and then for the first time ever, he admitted, "Beelzebub, I have to admit, I am confused. What would be best, I think, is for Him to die short of the cross. Part of the time, I think we would be better off if He chose to quit without dying, but then I fear Him reigning forever on Earth. Somehow, I have the feeling that He has won if He dies on a cross, but nothing could be worse than if He lives and reigns forever right here! I guess I'll let our orders to our forces stand as they are."

Morning was getting close, and Peter, being rather apprehensive, walked out on the porch. As he stepped out, someone spoke to him. When he answered, everyone looked up. One man said, "Hello—you must be one of Jesus's disciples. You sure sound Galilean!"

"You bet," someone else added, "I saw him in the garden."

Now, Peter was terrified. He began to curse and swear, "Man, I don't know what you're talking about. I've never seen the Guy before!"

Beelzebub, who had returned to badger Peter, nudged a Roman soldier, and said, "Really blow it, pal!"

The soldier raised the trumpet to his lips and blew a mighty blast. This denoted the changing of the guard, and was called 'The Crowing of the Cock', by the Jews. This was the second time the trumpet had been blown since Jesus had told Peter that he would deny Him three times before the second crowing of the cock.

Peter was crushed. Oh, how well he remembered Jesus's words. He could also remember so well his own boasting. He had failed utterly! How awful he felt!

Rushing headlong out into the yard, he collapsed and cried like a 200-pound baby.

The morning progressed until it was felt that Pontius Pilate would be up, and it would be permissible to take Jesus to him. The self-righteous Scribes and Pharisees wouldn't go into Pilate's judgment hall. That would ceremonially defile them, even as they were spiritually defiling themselves by trying to get the Son of God executed—murdered in cold blood! Satan had certainly sold them a bill of goods!

Judas had been watching the whole process. Now as it became obvious to him that Jesus wasn't going to perform some miracle and escape, he began to have second thoughts. He hadn't really, down in his heart, thought that Jesus would let them do this. Also, since Satan was through with him, the demons backed off and left him looking at himself for the first time. Now he really saw what an awful creature he actually was.

"Man you are such a cruddy creep that you don't even deserve to live. Do you slither along on your belly in slime? You've actually killed the Son of God! There's no hope for you now!" Ug told him.

Rushing back to the temple, he tried to buy Jesus back. "Here is your money. I have betrayed an innocent man. Turn Him loose!"

Now that they had no further use for him, the friendliness was gone. Caiaphas sneered, "Tough luck, fella, you made your bed, now it looks like you will just have to sleep in dirty sheets."

Judas threw down the thirty pieces of silver, ran blindly out of the temple, and on down the street.

Satan was alarmed. God had a way of forgiving people that he thought he had dead to rights. "Destroy him!" he ordered.

Judas's mind was in such a turmoil that he didn't even know how he got in the garden. The demons who controlled him did though. Shortly, however, he found himself beside a large, gnarled old tree that leaned out at an angle. He was in the Garden of Gethsemane, very close to where he had betrayed his Lord!

"Climb the tree," suggested Ug. "What you've done is unforgivable. Life isn't worth living anymore."

Climbing up the long leaning trunk of the tree until he was some eight or ten feet above the ground, he removed the sash from his waist, and tied it to a limb. He formed a loop in the other end and placed it around his neck, then he slid from the trunk.

At first, he thought the sash had broken. There was something strange, however, about the way he was drifting to the ground. Looking up, he was shocked to see his own body swinging and jerking on the end of the line. He looked down at himself, and found that he did, indeed, have a body which looked like the one hanging on the limb. He could feel! Maybe this wouldn't be so bad after all.

Even as the thought occurred to him, his gaze picked up what at first looked like a large patch of mist. Next, he realized that the mist was alive! It was a living glob of mist! The top end of the mist formed the most hideous face he had ever seen. The mist smiled, but there was no humor in the smile. It was an awful, evil smile! Sharp, excruciating pain shot through his leg. He looked down, and this was no mist! The creature which bit him had a body similar to a lizard. Its head looked like it might have been taken from a weasel. But it was big! It was as big as he was.

The mist spoke, "Never mind Weasel Face. He likes Jews. He tastes them every chance he gets."

The creature turned him loose, and Judas looked at the spot. There wasn't even a red spot to mark where he had been bitten.

A deep croaking voice caused him to turn his head to see what was on that side of him. The creature had a body very similar to a huge bull frog. A scrap of cloth hung down below his hips. This was the only vestige of the former angel known as Droopy Drawers.

"We'll take re-e-eel good care of you!" Droopy told him.

The mist spoke again. "You are in Lucifer's realm now. Don't cross him. These guys were angels at one time. This is what he did to them for punishment. And don't worry about Droopy Drawers. The only way he will hurt you is talk you to death."

Judas looked at Droopy. He had little spindly legs and arms. His body was shaped like a large bean. He had no neck as such. His head was shaped like a frogs and just grew out of his shoulders. His mouth went clear around his head, and formed a stupid grin. A tongue too long for his mouth hung out of it.

"Let's go, Ug" Weasel said in his strange chirpy voice.

"The mist must be called Ug," thought Judas as the two horrible creatures grabbed him and took to the air behind Ug.

As they mounted up into the atmosphere, Judas knew a certain amount of fear of the height. Droopy's mouth had been going nonstop, and Judas had nearly quit listening to him. Now as they neared the Dead Sea, and began descending to it, he picked up what Droopy was saying, "All the gates to Hell are in water. Can you think of a better place than a dead sea to have one?"

Now, Judas knew true apprehension. They were diving straight at the water. Of course, it was hard for him to think in the spiritual realm. He was surprised when they entered the water without even a splash.

Deeper and deeper they sank into the ever darkening waters. At last, he could make out a dark spot on the bottom. As they approached it, he could tell it was a cave. More of the grotesque fallen angels snarled at them as they entered. Now they plunged ever deeper into the cavern. Strange lights gleamed at intervals. Abruptly, a stone wall could be seen blocking their way.

Droopy's mouth was still going even in the water and he

said, "You have heard of the gates to Hell? That is what this is. Once you go through it, there is no return."

When they hit the wall at full speed, Judas expected to simply be smashed. Such was not the case. They penetrated it with ease, however, the pain was absolutely excruciating.

"See why you will never go back through there?" asked Droopy.

The next thing he knew, Judas was in the flames of Hades. He could actually see the myriads of demons who tormented him. Standing there glaring down at him was mighty Apollyon. There were still wounds on his face, wounds which would be there eternally, which DA had inflicted when he defeated him and took him to the Abyss. Judas just thought suicide would end his problems.

Suddenly, he discovered that he was lying on something very hot—frying hot! He looked down and saw that he was lying on a large flat rock. Steam rose from cracks in it and what looked like liquid flames lapped at the shore along side of him. Before he could look up, Apollyon kicked him in the side hard enough to give him the sensation of having the wind knocked out of him. Next his head jerked as Apollyon yanked him up by his hair. The big fallen angel then grasped him by an arm and a leg and twirled him around him as he spun on one foot. When released, Judas sailed out over the boiling flames before plunging into them. Searing pain! Unbelievable pain! He waited to die. He wished to die. He couldn't die! Abruptly, it dawned on him. He was dead and could live in this stuff indefinitely while in this state!

"Jesus! Save me! I'm so sorry for what I did!"

Apollyon's laughter was more nearly a shriek. "Too late! Judas! Too late! You should have thought of that before you sold the Son of God! You should have even thought of that before you slid from that tree trunk! Now you're mine!" Apollyon ended his little speech with another fiendish laugh.

The time had come to take Jesus to Pilate. Again, it was huge Malchus who took Him by the arm and led Him out into the street. Malchus couldn't help feeling a little sorry for Him.

Already much of His beard had been pulled out, and a good portion of His hair. One eye was swelled until it was just a slit, and His face was puffy. His lip was split open until it would cause trouble speaking. A long gash showed where a large ring had traveled along His cheek.

Satan's demon controlled followers were having a hay day! One rib ached from a foot placed in His side, but here too, Satan had lost. God would not allow a bone to be broken. No matter how hard the Devil drove his men, they would never do anything that God forbade!

Pilate was surprised when he saw the mob heading his way. This was one day on which he thought the Jews would be too busy celebrating to have any legal problems.

Mob madness was starting to get out of hand, and the Lord was hardly touching the ground as they approached Pilate.

Jesus was thrown unceremoniously at Pilate's feet. The ruler himself, could hardly tell what the charges they brought against Him were.

"Order!" he shouted, "Quiet down or I'll call the guard!"

When he could finally hear them, he was surprised at the seriousness of the charges.

The rulers of the Jews, the very agitators who hated Rome and didn't even believe in paying taxes to Caesar, were accusing this Guy of perverting the nation. The charges were that He had forbidden the Jews to pay tribute to the crown, and had said He was Christ Jesus, Himself a king.

Turning to Jesus, who was standing now, he asked, "Are You then, the king of the Jews?"

"Absolutely," answered Jesus.

Turning back to the Chief Priest's party, Pilate stated, "There is no law against being heir to the throne. I find no crime has been committed."

"He has stirred the people from here to Galilee," answered a florid faced Sadducee of rank.

Pilate looked up with interest, "Oh, is He a Galilean then?"

"Sure," sneered a nattily dressed Pharisee who might have been called 'Pretty Boy', "that is where all such scum comes from, isn't it?" Dandy, his own private demon, came as near smiling as a demon can, and thought, "Now, that's my man!"

Pilate looked the guy up and down in a manner that made his distaste obvious, and answered, "If you are so smart, why did you bring Him to me. He belongs in Herod's jurisdiction. Take Him to Herod!" So saying, he turned and strode away.

As Herod was in Jerusalem for the feast, this was no problem for the Jews. Jesus was simply hazed and abused from Pilate's Judgment Hall to where Herod and his troops were lodged.

Herod was genuinely pleased to see Jesus. He had heard a great deal about Him, and he hoped Jesus would perform some spectacular miracle for him.

"Ah, so You are Jesus, The Messiah, King of the Jews," he mocked. "Well, Mr. Christ King, perform a great big miracle of some kind for me, and I'll turn You loose. I'll even send a squad of soldiers to make sure that no one bothers You."

"Hey Man! That's just what You've been looking for!" whispered Rege. "God has supplied You with Your way out! Isn't He good? Perform his miracle. All his soldiers will believe in You. A lot of good will come of it, and You'll be turned loose without having to die!"

"Don't do it, Lord! You'll just be handing the Devil the keys to the store!" DA almost shouted to His mind.

DA needn't have worried.

Harod had been watching Jesus intently. It was said that Jesus was John the Baptist raised from the dead. It had been he, Herod, who had beheaded John. If this really was John risen from the dead, it just might be time for him to exit the scene as fast as his short pudgy legs could take him. As he watched, however, he became convinced that this wasn't John. Now, any fears he might have had swiftly melted.

The Chief Priest's party was really laying it on Jesus. Pretty Boy's high pitched voice could be heard above everyone else's, "He's done everything from high treason to consorting with harlots!" he squeaked.

Jesus merely stood there looking Herod in the eye and saying nothing.

"Nothing to say, eh?" queried Herod with an evil glint in his eye. Turning to the soldiers, he said, "Have fun, fellas, He's all yours for a while."

Satan's mind was in a turmoil. Part of the time he wanted Jesus to quit and choose to live out of God's will, then he would want Him killed at any cost. Now he had hoped that Christ would leap at the chance that Herod gave Him to avoid the cross. Since He hadn't, the devil would use the demon controlled and possessed Roman soldiers to throw a temper tantrum.

A heavy jowled, hooked nosed centurion drove a mailed fist into Christ's midsection. When He doubled up, another soldier laid the flat of a sword to His back side with such strength that it straightened Him up again.

This type of torture continued until they tired of it. Then, borrowing one of Herod's scarlet robes, they dressed Him up like royalty and pretended to reverence Him as they would a great king.

This was no accident. Satan was in full control now. He wanted to show Christ how bad he could make it, and what He was giving up. How much easier it would be to accept the robe and a crown and become king now, without the horror of the crucifixion. Satan's mind was getting to be in even more of a turmoil by the minute. One minute the thought of Jesus living and reigning on Earth forever terrified him. The next, the thought that Jesus was ready and willing to be crucified scared him even more. If He didn't die, somehow, man would be unsaved. Perhaps if He reigned over unsaved people, Satan would still have won.

He had reckoned without the physical as well as spiritual strength of Christ. This man was no weakling! He could take it!

After going through the agony of the garden, He was actually glorying in every phase of His strength. He was a man among men! Already, He was barely recognizable; however, there wasn't the slightest hint of faltering. The saints of all ages would be saved!

Would you believe, it was the Scribes and Pharisees who

ended this portion of His abuse? Satan's control is not absolute! The priests didn't want Him beaten to death! They wanted Him alive on a cross! Death on a cross could take days, and this is what they wanted—revenge!

Herod, doubtlessly thinking back to the beheading of John, didn't want this man's blood on his hands too. He ordered, "This is Pilate's city. Take Him back to him. I'll abide by his decision."

Pilate really wasn't happy when Jesus was brought back. He thought he had gotten around this rather sticky problem when he sent Him to Herod.

"All right," he began in a very stern and unhappy manner, "Do you want to bring formal charges against Him, and what are they? We have to think of the legal side of this, you know."

The priests returned, "If He wasn't a criminal, we wouldn't have brought Him to you. Sure we want to bring charges against Him!"

"In that case," answered Pilate, "I give you permission to take Him and try Him according to your own laws."

"We would," they answered, "however, we can't put Him to death."

"Oh my aching head, this is getting worse as it goes along!" he thought. Turning around, he went back into the judgment hall and began to question Jesus. "Are You really the King of the Jews?" he asked. If only this Guy would give him something to use to free Him with! It was obvious that the Chief Priest's party was simply jealous of Him and trying to use the Roman courts to do their dirty work. He didn't like that a bit!

Finally, through bruised and broken lips, Christ replied, "Is this really your own question, or are you simply parroting what the Chief Priest and Scribes have been saying?"

Pilate shook his head in irritation and answered, "Do I look like a Jew, Fellow? Your own people are screaming for Your blood. What in the world have You done to build such a fire in them?"

"OK," Jesus began through His painful mouth with its normally white teeth gleaming red from the blood. "My kingdom is not of this world. I am interested in man's soul; not his body as far as ruling him is concerned. If My kingdom had been an earthly one, you have no idea how much pressure My servants could bring to bear to deliver Me from the Jews."

As He spoke, His mind went back to the mighty Michael, that He had so recently been speaking to. Continuing, He added, "My kingdom, however, is spiritual not earthly."

Thoughtfully, Pilate queried, "You are a king, though, huh?"

"Sure," answered Jesus, "that is why I was born. One of My main reasons for being on Earth is to witness to the truth."

Pilate's reaction was typically worldly. He replied, "Truth?" and with a snort, added, "What is truth?"

My, this was getting rough. Pilate was a man of conscience, and this was beginning to look more like cold-blooded murder to him. Murder even if it was done in a legal manner.

While these thoughts were running through his mind, a messenger from his wife arrived. The message read: "Honey, I have had a dream—I believe it was a vision. It was about this Jesus. You mustn't let any harm come to Him!"

Oh—! Why did things have to keep going from bad to worse? Ah-h-h! A ray of hope! Why hadn't he thought of it sooner? He hit his feet and strode out to speak to the Jews.

"Attention now, folks. I find absolutely no fault in Jesus. Since we have a custom of turning a prisoner loose each year at this time, I will release your king to you!"

"Look fella," they replied, "we don't have any king except Caesar, and you better not either!" The threat in their voice was real, and Pilate couldn't miss it.

"All right then, who do you want released?"

"Barabbas!" they shouted in unison.

Pilate was thunderstruck. Of all the prisoners he could think of, Barabbas was the last man he would have supposed that they would have asked for. Barabbas! Murderer, thug, you name it, he had done it! He was in every way a man of violence! Well, it stood to reason when you looked at it. They were trying to kill a man who was just the opposite.

"OK, OK, then what do you want me to do with Jesus which is called Christ?"

In a swelling roar, they cried, "Crucify Him!"

When the noise subsided enough to be heard, he shouted, "Why folks? What has He done? I've just told you that I can find no fault in Him! I'm going to punish Him and turn Him loose."

So saying, he did a military about face, went back inside where he gave orders for Jesus to be whipped, and then went on to other matters.

Jesus knew that David had prophesied that one would be able to see every bone in His body[17]. He thought with a certain amount of detachment that He was about to see that portion of scripture fulfilled.

Pilate hoped in the mean time that the crowd would disperse so he could quietly release Jesus.

The soldiers were rather careful in removing Jesus's clothing, for they knew that if He were crucified, they would get them. However, thereafter all resemblance of gentleness was absent.

His hands were roughly lashed to a large stake. Why be careful? He's the same as dead anyway, isn't He?"

A large Ethiopian slave stepped up. He wore only a loin cloth, and his muscles bulged as he moved. In his hands was the vicious Roman Cat-O-Ninetails. It was a handle with literally nine whips on it, and the lashes ended with metal and bone barbs. The punishment for not applying it hard enough was to have it used on oneself.

Rege threw a surge of unholy fear into the slave, and the huge man applied the whip with vigor! Forty lashes were considered the death penalty, but this whipping wouldn't stop at forty lashes. Rege would spur the big slave on. He would whip the Lord until, as Jesus had foreseen, His chest would be a fleshless ribcage. All His other bones would at some place, gleam white in the morning light. Still, God would not allow His perfect sacrifice to die any other way than that which He had foretold!

When the whipping was over, scripture was fulfilled. Jesus was whipped and beaten beyond recognition. Almost, He didn't even look human! The demon possessed soldiers; however, were not through. Again, He was dressed as royalty, and this time, He would have a crown. It was built out of long poisonous thorns, and driven down upon His head. He was dressed in the ultimate—royal purple! After this, the soldiers continued to beat and torture Him just for the pure sport of it! Oh yes, to the demon possessed, that is sport!

Satan thought that surely, by now, He must be about ready to call upon His angelic army and give up, leaving man without a savior. Not my Jesus! That day, He stood a man among men!

Pilate, looking at Him, thought certainly, the Jews, seeing one of their own in such a pitiful condition, would be overcome with pity, and allow him to release Him. Such was not the case. There were demons and fallen angels aplenty to go around out in the crowd, and they were all beside themselves.

Pilate led the shambling wreck out onto the balcony, and the crowd went wild. "Crucify Him, Crucify Him!"

"Why? What law has He broken?"

"He broke our law when He made Himself out to be the Son of God," they returned.

Pilate was a superstitious man. Upon hearing that, his face went pale. Leading Jesus back into the hall, he asked, "Man, Who and What are You? Where did you come from?"

Jesus, for several reasons, didn't even bother answering him. For one thing, it wasn't going to do any good. For another, He hurt so badly that breathing or moving His lips was just pure agony. His silence was foretold in scripture, and He could certainly understand the prophecy in another light now.

In his frustration, Pilate was becoming angry. "Look Fella, I have the power to either crucify You or not so You had better answer me!"

This man was beginning to get to him. As long as He was just some weird character with illusions of grandeur, and wild ideas about a kingdom that didn't exist, that was one thing. If however, He really was a God in the spiritual kingdom—now that was scary!

Wearily, Jesus answered him, "Aw knock it off, Pilate, you haven't got any power that hasn't been given you from above. Your sin is bad enough; however, he who handed Me over to you has the graver sin."

Now, Pilate was frightened, and determined to turn Him loose. He stepped back out and faced the crowd, which was growing more ugly by the minute. "Listen," he shouted, "neither Herod nor I have found any fault in this Man. I'm going to turn Him loose!"

The crowd shouted back, "Listen yourself, Pilate. He made Himself king. Thus He can't be Caesar's friend, and neither can you, if you befriend Him!"

Wow! Where do you go from here? Behind him is a man who may be a God. In front of him is the reality of an angry Caesar! Being a Roman soldier, he was much more frightened of Caesar.

"Bring me a basin of water!" he ordered. When it arrived, he washed his hands and told the people, "I am innocent of this just man's blood. You are witnesses!"

They answered, "Let His blood be upon us and upon our children!"

"So be it!" Pilate snapped, as he turned and motioned to the squad that would be in charge of the crucifixion.

The iron clad soldiers stepped forward and led Jesus away to begin the final phase of His earthly ministry.

Pilot looked down at his hands as he walked back into the hall, and they appeared to be covered with blood!

CHAPTER XV

THE CROSS

The soldiers led Jesus out into the bright morning sunlight. It was a time that Jesus normally, would have loved for its beauty and purity. However, this morning, He was looking at it through feverish, pain racked eyes.

Since He had to put up with a human body such as ours, He concentrated upon the job at hand. He dared make no mistake, or all would be lost. He had taken enough punishment to kill Him, yet He lived. He had taken far more pain than the two thieves who would die with Him. Still He stumbled on, prodded with the butt end of a spear.

The Jewish hecklers would have liked to have gotten to Jesus along the way; however, the tough Roman soldiers didn't care any more for the people than they did for Jesus. In fact, this gutty heir to the Jewish throne was winning their grudging respect. He was beginning to show them what kings should be made of. The people met only a wall of spear points.

Tough though Jesus was, when the heavy cross timber was dropped upon His shoulders, His rubbery legs almost went out from under Him. From somewhere deep within, a spurt of raw will power came to His rescue, and He staggered off toward the hill.

A big strong fellow who was in the crowd, seeing Jesus's condition, stepped out fearlessly in case the obviously weakening Jesus should falter. Jesus collapsed before Simon got there, and Simon the Cyrenian found himself being ordered forward at spear point.

He would go down in history as having the distinction of being the man who carried Jesus's cross to Calvary for Him. Simon counted it a privilege. He would be remembered by the first century Christians as a brave man and a hero.

As is often the case, the crowd of the night before, was a minority. Now, even at this early hour, a large crowd began to assemble. They were weeping and lamenting as they went along.

Jesus, weary though He was, couldn't help looking down through time and seeing the anguish that the Jewish people would go through before He came back. No, not for crucifying Him, for rejecting Him. "Don't weep for Me, ladies," He told them. "Weep for yourselves, for the day is coming when you'll wish you had never been born!"

Simon dragged the heavy cross beam up to three solidly set posts that had taken part in this demon ritual many times before. They stood on the very crest of Golgotha. Appropriately enough, Golgotha means the Place of the Skull. After positioning the beam close to the center post, he was allowed to drop it. Christ viewed the cross with mixed emotions. He was so fatigued that in a sense, it was a relief to be able to stop. However, it was with gut gripping horror that He lay down and stretched out His hands.

Once more, the soldiers had to respect His raw courage. It appeared that at least this was one man they weren't going to have to wrestle down. My, what a soldier He would have made if He had been on their side!

Ropes were brought after His hands were nailed to the cross beam, and they tied Him to it to support His weight as they raised Him into place. This was done so the nails wouldn't pull through while they fastened the cross beam to the upright one.

He was seated so He sat upon a triangular block, which sloped down. One foot was placed upon another such block with the second foot on top of the first.

A huge square, rusty spike was placed against the top

foot and pointed so it would go through both feet at about the same spot. It was about a half inch thick, its sides were anything but smooth, and its point lacked a great deal of being sharp.

A big, burly soldier, who obviously had been in on many crucifixions, swung a heavy mall a very expert blow. The nail penetrated both feet and went quite a ways into the block.

A cry escaped Jesus's lips this time. The next two blows that it took to drive the spike in far enough to suit the soldier, however, only wrung grimaces of anguish from Him.

His feet were so close to the ground as He hung on the cross that loved ones and friends had to keep the wild dogs back so they wouldn't tear His flesh.

Satan said to his followers, "It's O.K., men, He may be God, but He has a human body. No human being can stand to be crucified if he can help it, and He can help it. Any moment now, He'll call for Michael, and somehow, because He didn't die, and we forced God to change His plan, man will be lost forever."

But He did take it. The nails were not through the fleshly center of His hands, that would tear to easily. They were right where the wrist joins the hand, and my friend, that hurt! Satan had every reason to believe as he did, but he was wrong!

Mary writhed as she sobbed into John's comforting shoulder, "I can almost imagine what that must feel like. Yet, really I know I can't. Oh, my poor Baby!"

For one blessed moment, Jesus passed out. Then reality came back in a rush. From now on, each breath would be bought with a price. A breath was impossible as long as one hung as these men did. They would have to lunge up for each short gasp of air, raw backs scraping against the rough wood.

No; suicide was out, for muscles would cramp and the body would convulse enough to get sufficient air to live. Christ had made it this far; however, Satan still didn't think He could take it long enough to die. Men had been known to live for weeks this way!

In the midst of His own agony, Jesus couldn't help thinking of the punishment, which was coming to these people. He cried out, "Father forgive them, for they know not what they do!"

Jesus watched the soldiers give wine mixed with myrrh to the man next to Him. The man got high and then seemed to go into a stupor. When they brought Him His, He said, "Thanks, but no thanks."

The soldier just shrugged his shoulders, and went on to the next. If Jesus didn't want anything to ease the pain, he couldn't care less. Jesus, on the other hand, was going to need all His faculties, and that firewater didn't look like the answer.

To kill time, the soldiers began to divide up Christ's clothes. Rather than tear it, they gambled for His one piece robe. They had them all divided up by nine o'clock. That wasn't a bad day's work.

Above Jesus's head was a sign written in Hebrew, Greek, and Latin: JESUS OF NAZARETH, THE KING OF THE JEWS!

"Pilate! How could you possibly give that felon such a title?! You must write, 'He said, I'm the King of the Jews'."

Pilate turned and squinted at the fat Jew, and the hair on Caiaphas's neck stood on end.

In a voice which was deadly quiet, Pilate said, "Caiaphas, that sign says just what I want it to. Now, if you don't want one over your head, see that I don't see you for a long time!"

Pilate glanced at a guard, but before his escort could arrive, fat Caiaphas was scurrying for the door.

This was Jesus's enemies' day; however, and they made the most of it. "Oh, you bet!" They nodded their heads in agreement. "There is your Messiah, Israel!" they shouted gleefully.

One must admit, He didn't look the part with all His hair and beard pulled out by the roots, His face beaten beyond recognition, and the flesh whipped from His bones. Had they known the scriptures, they would have read where they would do these things to Him in Isaiah chapters 50-53 and Psalms 22.

"Yah Man! You were going to rebuild the temple in three days, and now You can't even come down from the cross, King of Israel! Save Yourself, Big Man!"

Even fat, pudgy old Annas and Caiaphas waddled up the hill. They puffed and panted as they gloated over Him for a while. "How can a man save others when He can't even save Himself? Come on down from the cross, Your Majesty, and we'll believe on You! He trusted in God. Now if God will have Him, let's see Him deliver Him!"

Rege thought, "If He's got a weak moment, this has to be it!" Then he whispered to Jesus, "Man, You are a mess! If You did come down from the cross and stand before them perfectly healed, they would fall at Your feet. They'd be afraid not to!"

Jesus had left all His weaknesses in the garden. Now He never even let the thought slow down. It passed right on through His mind without hesitation. Rege could only marvel at this Being, and dreaded facing Lucifer.

One thief took it up and said, "Look Mister, if You aren't a phoney, and are Christ, save Yourself and us!"

The other spoke up, "Careful, pal, don't you even fear God? We're getting what we have coming, but this poor Guy hasn't done anything to deserve this."

Then, speaking to Jesus, he said, "Lord, remember me when You come into your kingdom."

Right there, two thieves had a parting of the ways. One would go to Paradise, and the other to The Place of Torment, for Jesus was touched by the one thief's faith.

He turned His head painfully, and replied, "Pal, this is a promise. This day, we'll stroll through Paradise together."

Jesus's eye fell upon His beloved John standing near by consoling Mary. Again, His heart was touched. Nothing blustery about the guy, but he had the guts to stand right up alongside the cross, and let the chips fall where they may.

Speaking to His mother, He said, "Woman, John will take My place as your son since I'll be gone."

Then speaking to John, "My friend, treat her just like your own mother."

"She'll spend the rest of her life in my home, Master. That's a promise."

At the beginning of the sixth hour—noon, an unnatural darkness settled over the land. It would serve several purposes. It would shield Jesus from the blistering sun. It would demonstrate God's power, and it would cause the hair on the back of the necks of the ungodly to stand right on end. Many would find something else to do for a while, beside heckle Jesus!

It's effect would also be profound upon Jesus, for now God would make Him to be sin who knew no sin. The sins of us all would be placed upon Jesus and judged. Since God can't look upon sin, for the first time ever, God would turn His back upon Jesus. Jesus would cry, "Eli, Eli, lama sabachthani?" which means, "My God, My God, why have you forsaken Me?"

The bystanders thought He was calling for Elijah, and when one was going to offer Him some of the drugged hooch, another ordered, "Wait a minute. Let's see if Elijah does come to rescue Him."

Jesus knew now that all was fulfilled, and asked for a drink. He was handed a sponge filled with the pain killing drug.

After merely a taste, He spoke out so that the whole world would know, "It is finished!" After a pause, He shouted, "Father, into Your hands I commend My Spirit!"

Satan and all the demons in Hell shuddered. The body that should have died from its beatings, but could have lived for days on the cross—did die now. The weakened heart that they had tried so hard to destroy in the garden, now, mercifully, was allowed to rupture. Jesus died of a broken heart, just as God planned. Satan leaned back and a look of relief crossed his face. "At least now, He'll never be able to reign over Israel here on Earth. We have won that much."

The priests should have known now, if there really were any doubts in their minds, that they had been in error. The massive four inch thick veil of the temple split from top to bottom. This showed that the way to God was now open to all. Man could come directly to God for forgiveness without a human priest or sacrifice. As if this wasn't enough, the earth quaked, stones split, and lightening flashed.

The Jews may not have believed; however, the pagan Roman centurion did. He cried, "Surely, this was the Son of God!"

All of the Sanhedrin weren't bad. One man named Joseph of Arimathaea counted himself amongst Jesus's disciples. He came to Pilate and asked, "Sir, may I have the body of Jesus so I can bury it before the Sabbath?"

Pilate was suspicious and somewhat surprised, "Are you sure He is dead this soon?"

"Yes Sir," Joseph assured him.

Pilate was still unconvinced, and turned to his own private messenger, "Go tell the centurion to break all the men's legs. Be sure they are dead before taking them down. Then he is to give Jesus to Joseph for burial."

The courier saluted and ran from the building.

The breaking of the men's legs was an act of mercy, for then they couldn't breathe. For some, this would end days of suffering.

Now, Satan was hoping for even a minor victory. Scripture says that there wouldn't be any of Christ's bones broken. He might have known though, that he couldn't win.

The two thieves, of course, had to have their legs broken, but Christ was obviously dead. A man's legs are hard to break, even with heavy weapons, when he is hanging on a cross. The easy route was to stick a spear in His side, which, indeed, was foretold. This also, let out the blood mixed with water, which proved beyond a doubt, that He was not only dead, but that He had died of a broken (ruptured) heart, a heart attack!

The body was then given to Joseph and Nicodemus, who too, had stepped out to take his stand now. They wrapped Him in linen strips and literally plastered Him with a hundred pounds of moist spices. He was virtually wearing an aromatic cast, whose fumes, themselves, would have smothered Him had He still been alive. Except for His face, which was not wrapped, He looked like an Egyptian mummy.

Joseph placed Jesus in his own new grave, which had never been used. He then covered the only part of Him which was not casted, His face, with a linen kerchief.

Next, with the help of a crowd of men who were Jesus's followers, they rolled a stone weighing many tons against the door and went their way.

Above was only blackness. Welcome to the land of the dead! Below stretched a yawning canyon with apparently no bottom. As one descended, it too was only darkness, a blackness beyond human comprehension. If one had descended far enough, pale faces looking up would have appeared. Strange flying objects would have flitted around—fallen cherubim. Bottom bound fallen angels with haunted faces staring up, never quite giving up hope, even when there was no hope. Ethereal objects floated around—demons damned here with the rest for evilness or crimes which were so bad that they couldn't be allowed on earth. Fallen angels under the iron control of Apollyon! Welcome to the Abyss! Tartarus! Hell's maximum security facility! The Bottomless Pit!

On one side, at the top of this monstrous cavern, stretched boiling liquid flame—a lake of it! Yes, this is the abode of fallen, unsaved man since the time of Adam! Yes, Cain is there, still cooking! People screamed, and begged, crying—to no avail. Their only hope was for Satan to win—and He had just lost! Oh, the price of rejecting salvation so freely given! Oh yes, the Rich Man who had abused Lazarus—he's still there too!

Across from the Abyss—Oh! How beautiful! Paradise! Abraham's Bosom[18]   Matthew 10:28 says to fear him who is capable of destroying both body and soul. This destruction will occur in the Lake of Fire, after The Great White Throne Judgment. The body will be the first to die, then according to their evil deeds, their soul will survive until justice is done. Then, their spirit, which is similar to those of the Pre-adamic man, will survive eternally in torment and separation from God. These spirits are described in Job 4:14-21.! Grass greener than any on Earth. This was the only part of Hades with true light. On the other side of the Abyss there was only the eerie, flickering light of the flames. But on this side, flowers which were more beautiful and sweeter smelling than ever caressed the nostrils of mortal man awaited the entrance of the saved from Earth! No need, yea, no want denied these who had chosen to follow Jehovah God.

For the first time, the darkness above Hades was rent by blinding light. Christ led a wedge of Heaven's finest. He was now a two-part being as the rest of those in Hades were, being absent from His body, and consisting of Soul and Spirit. Behind Him came Michael and Gabriel. After them came DA, Raphael, Caleb, and the whole fighting Seventh Legion.

On one side of the great gulf, the hordes of Hell were simply abject. On the other side, Abraham's Bosom, pandemonium reigned! People were shouting for joy! Some were weeping as wonderful emotions gripped their souls. They were laughing, waving their arms—pure joy! Yes, Adam and Eve welcoming the Seed of The Woman into their arms!

Christ halted His descent above the Abyss, where all could see and hear him from all three compartments. His emotions all but choked Him as He looked around. His gaze took in the boiling lake, and sorrow gripped His soul.

"First, to those who are lost," He said, "to those who have chosen to follow Satan. Oh how My heart breaks. You are still lost, and will be for eternity. There is nothing that can be done for you. I have won, and Satan has lost. Those who have lived a life of rebellion have bought eternity in Hell. You were not forced to go there. By your acts, you have chosen to go there. I'm so sorry——"

Turning to face Abraham's Bosom, His face lit up. "—but to all who have lived Godly lives during the Old Testament period, and those who will accept Me as Savior during the New Testament period—we have won! I died a death I didn't deserve, since I was sinless. Hence, My undeserved death bought your undeserved life. From now on, salvation will be either free or unobtainable. It will be obtainable only through Me."

While Jesus was preaching in Hell, the Chief Priest, Scribes, Pharisees, and Sadducees, as well as their hangers on, were making further preparation to go there some day. A couple of them were gloating over their victory, and one happened to remember something.

"Say, didn't that imposter say that He would rise after three days?"

"Boy, that's right. If someone should steal that body, we could be in worse trouble than we ever were. They would say He has risen; and it's pretty hard to fight a man who isn't even there!"

Shortly, they were voicing their fears to Caiaphas, who sent them on to Pilate.

"Sir, that imposter said He would rise on the third day. We fear that His disciples will steal His body. The final result would be worse than before."

Pilate wasn't impressed; however, he commanded, "O.K., set a watch and seal the tomb with my signet."

As quickly as they could get the less than excited guards together, the tomb was secured by a crack squad of Roman soldiers. Believe me—no one was going to steal this body!

A demon appeared at Satan's side, so fresh from Hades that one could almost see the sparks on him and smell the smoke. "Master! I have a message from Apollyon! All Hell is in an uproar! Jesus is claiming victory, and saying He will rise from the dead!"

"Victory? How could He claim victory?" asked Beelzebub.

"I can see it now," moaned Satan. "If He rises from the dead, He can still rule."

"He also says He has paid for the sins of those who accept Him," added the imp. "He says they can be saved without being perfect!"

"No one can be saved without being perfect," Satan said explosively. "They have to earn their salvation! They have to do perfect works! They have to keep the law perfectly, which no one can do!"

"Not anymore," the imp said as he vanished from the scene. He felt almost glad to be headed back to Hell.

Satan sat silently for a while, and Beelzebub knew better than to say anything. Almost as if waking from a doze, Satan snapped, "IF—if He rises from the dead. He has to rise to make it work! He hasn't risen yet! Beelzebub, get all our forces around that tomb!"

Back in Hades, the unpleasant portion of His duties finished, Christ moved on to Abraham's Bosom.

"Lord, I have had so many unanswered questions for so many thousands of years. I have so looked forward to visiting with You. Now the day has finally come," Abraham said.

Jesus knew that it was going to take no small period of time, just to greet and visit with all of the old saints dating back to Adam and Eve. Some would have to wait until they were in Heaven's Paradise. There were certain questions that would be relevant to all. These He answered for the multitude, before dealing with those He had time for.

First of all, He explained sacrifices. "Beloved, you had to sacrifice perfect, innocent animals because I am perfect and innocent—sinless. The sacrifices had to die just as I had to die. The big difference is, I will rise!" Motioning to Adam and Eve, He said, "Even their clothes were taken from an innocent animal. The death of the animal, and its skin that covered their naked bodies symbolized my death that covered their sin. Another difference is that the animals had to be offered over and over again, where I died once for all. The innocent animal's death, dying for your guilt, did temporarily, what My unearned death did for eternity. The innocent lamb was actually sort of a picture of Me"

It was easy for them to see, now, that the dying animal wouldn't have accomplished anything if Jesus hadn't died as well. The dying animal was simply a picture of the death of Christ. Too, the animal wasn't sufficient for it couldn't rise. Christ had to rise to make His own death worth anything. In fact, if Jesus hadn't died, the death of the animal would have been worthless.

In a way, the Old Testament people had been saved by grace, just as the New Testament ones would be. They had been looking forward to His death, while we look back at it. As Satan had seen, however, none of it would be worth anything if He didn't rise from the dead!

There was also no small stir when He said, "Beloved, when I arise from the dead, I shall take you with Me to Paradise in Heaven. The wicked will be left here, and the Place of Torment will be expanded to include at least most of the rest of the area."

The Jews were quite familiar with the Temple structure, and he continued to explain, "Paradise is the equivalent of the Holy Place in the Temple. You won't have access to the Holy of Holies—The Throne Room—until you receive your resurrection bodies at the Second Coming. Paradise will be much better than Abraham's Bosom, and you will have access to Me there. The saved Christians will also go there until the Rapture rings down the curtain on the Christian Church."

Time simply flew until it was time for Christ to arise.

CHAPTER XVI

RESURRECTION

The time in Hades drew to a close, and now it was time to complete the defeat of Satan. Christ must arise from the dead! Shortly after His resurrection, many old saints would be allowed to rise and go to Paradise in their resurrection bodies after visiting throughout the city.

Ancient History has it that Adam knew where Christ would arise and had his and Eve's bodies buried there. It is possible that they were among those given this privilege.

In the stratosphere above Jerusalem, the Chariot of God, seen by both Ezekiel, Isaiah, and the Apostle John in Revelation, hovered, waiting for the Old Testament saints.

Satan's forces were in position for battle; however, they had little or no heart for it. Heaven's forces, spearheaded by the chariots of fire and the warrior cherubim, hit them, hard! The battle was over without it even really getting started. A few more of Satan's angels would die and simply become disembodied spirits for eternity.

Lazing around in the morning sun by the tomb, completely unaware of the savage, but very short battle that was taking place in the atmosphere around them, a squad of Roman soldiers were really enjoying their tour of duty.

"How long do you suppose they'll have us watch this Old Boy's bones?" one of them queried.

"Hey fella," another one whose baby face belied the tough soldier within the suit of Roman armor cut in. "Be a little careful what you say. I was in on the crucifixion detail. There is something about this Guy that kind of makes your skin crawl. Even the centurion that day said he thought He might actually be the Son of God. If I really believed He said He was going to rise again, I'd put in for a transfer!"

"Be my guest," said a large fellow with a broken nose and a scar running at an angle across his face. As far as I'm concerned, I think I'll hang around for a while. Besides, I can't believe He'll be rising from the dead," he added, rising to stretch.

In a motion of pure fluid grace, his Roman broad sword appeared in his hand looking like a flash of light. It cut a vicious arc at an imaginary foe, and returned to its sheath.

A look of satisfaction crossed his face as he commented, "I'd like to see the man, or a dozen of them, for that matter, who could take this body from me!"

He had just started to sit down again, when a light brighter than the sun gleamed around them. A man who could, indeed, take whatever he wanted away from all of them, appeared, standing by the stone. DA gave the scarred soldier a bemused grin. Effortlessly, and with one hand, he reached out and rolled back the stone that had all but stymied as many men as could get around it when they were trying to roll it down hill. He then nonchalantly sat upon the stone, completely ignoring the Roman soldiers who were literally paralyzed with terror.

Inside the tomb, Michael and Gabriel were attending a third man, the risen Lord!

With a burst of energy, Jesus's body had changed from mortal to immortal and had come right through the heavy spice and linen cast without even disturbing it. He then, neatly folded the linen face cloth and laid it aside.

Christ left the freed Old Testament saints in the air above Jerusalem while He took part in His resurrection. The Chariot of God, the mighty throne on its diamond floor, with its brazen altar and the spectacular four faced cherubim inside the wheels within wheels literally hung in the space above. The risen saints lounged around on its floor. A cloud enveloped the throne, for at this point in time, they couldn't look upon the Father. In the future, He will call the risen and changed Christians up to Him to this same spot in the clouds at the Rapture. The chariot will pause there in its descent during the second coming of Christ. It will wait there during the Tribulation, before continuing on to Earth at the end of the seven years.

Things were beginning to happen fast now. Mary Magdalene, Mary, the mother of James, as well as Salome, Joanna, and others were approaching the tomb. Jesus wasn't quite ready to make His visible presence known to them, so He rendered Himself intangible and invisible. The crowd looked in and saw only the two angels who began to speak.

"O.K., ladies, why are you looking for the living amongst the dead? Go tell His disciples that Jesus has risen! Don't you remember that He said He would arise the third day? Oh, yes, and be sure to tell Peter in particular."

It was kind of a case of, "Oh yah, now I remember!"

The ladies were both amazed and afraid while being overjoyed. They all turned and ran to tell the disciples. All, that is, except Mary Magdalene. Poor Mary was both confused, shocked, and completely unable to grasp the sense of the whole thing. She wandered off weeping.

Jesus didn't really want to make Himself visible until after He completed His mission in Heaven. However, Mary was just breaking His heart, and He turned and came back to her.

"Why are you crying, Ma'am?" He asked, "Were you looking for someone?"

Mary, dazed and looking through tear filled eyes, didn't recognize Him. She mistook Him for the gardener or some other grounds keeper. She asked, "Sir, where have you taken Jesus? If You will only tell me, I'll gladly come and get Him!"

With aching heart, Jesus exclaimed, "Mary!" At this, she recognized Him and would have hugged Him as she cried, "Master!"

He, however eluded her and exclaimed, "Mary! Don't touch Me! I haven't ascended to Heaven. I must return to the Father, and then I'll meet you all down town later. When I get back, you can hug Me all you want to. Now go tell the others that you've seen Me."

With the exit of the last angel, the big Roman soldiers came out of their stupor, and they beat a hasty retreat.

At a safe distance, they stopped to think. Baby Face said, "We don't dare go back and tell the commander what happened. He won't believe us and we're all dead men! I told you this Guy was no one to mess with!"

"I think the only thing to do is go to the Chief Priest," suggested Scar Face. "Things look pretty bleak at best, but that seems like the lesser of the evils to me."

Actually, this was a very good move. Caiaphas believed them, and even if he had any doubts, this was a story that he didn't dare let get out. If these soldiers were killed, their story would spread. Everyone would believe that Jesus had risen from the dead. If He had done that, He was probably really the Christ.

If Caiaphas didn't squelch that story, he might easily be the next one decorating Jesus's cross. No Sir! The only thing he could do was pay these guys to tell the story he wanted told, and see that they didn't get into trouble for it.

Smiling as pleasantly as Caiaphas knew how, he ordered his treasurer, "Give these men a bag of money apiece, and then leave the room, Jacob."

"Ah, pardon me, Sir. Did you say, 'Give them a bag of money?'" the astonished man asked.

"Yes!" roared Caiaphas, and before he could say more, the man fled.

Caiaphas switched back to his sickeningly sweet manner and began, "Men, this is a very touchy situation. I hope I can depend upon your discretion. Tell everyone that you fell asleep, and the disciples stole His body. Don't worry about your commander. I'll tell him you are saying what I want you to say. Make it sound good, and there may be more well paying work for you sometime. O.K.?"

The soldiers could hardly believe this. One moment, they figured they were dead men, and here they were looking at more money than they would generally see in a year, maybe many years—and all they had done was fail!

"You better believe it!" chortled Scar Face, and Baby Face whispered in awe, "Oh, thank you, Sir!"

Meanwhile, Mary understood now, and she ran after them so hard that she overtook the rest, even after taking time to stop and tell Peter and John, whom she met on the trail: "Jesus has risen!"

At the same time, Jesus returned to the Old Testament saints, and in a moment of time, at the speed of thought, the Chariot of God, Jesus, the crew, and all the old saints were in the Eden of the Heavenly Paradise.

Jesus anointed it with the bloody touch of His nail pierced hand, and leaving the saints in the Holy Place, continued on to the Throne Room, which didn't show any sign that it had moved. Again, His bloody touch anointed all the furniture there, just as the blood of bulls anointed the tabernacle and its furniture on Earth.

Time was running out here too, as Jesus raced to keep up with the schedule that had caught Him up from the moment He died on the cross. Now He had to get back to Earth, but He did take time for a joyous reunion with those in the Throne Room.

With the anointing completed, Gabriel and Michael strolled with Jesus down to the River of Life. Jesus reached up and picked one of the luscious pieces of fruit from the tree of life and took a bite. Instantly, the blood dripping from his wounded hands dried up. Now, all that was left were the scars which He would wear as badges of His office for eternity. Then, in a moment of time, He was back on Earth.

After talking to Mary, big bold Peter took off at a run for the grave. John finished listening to Mary, and then too, began to run. He was more lithely built, and soon caught and passed Peter.

He was the first to reach the crypt, but years of training caused him to stop short of entering the defiling tomb. However, impulsive Peter never even slowed down before entering the now empty sepulcher.

With Peter's example, John too, walked on in to view the grave clothes. They were empty! And the linen wrappings formed a cast of Jesus's body, just like a plaster cast of a broken arm. The only difference was that the spices replaced the plaster of Paris.

But this cast was empty! And it had not been cut open! How do you get out of something like that? The only way was by rising from the dead as Jesus had!

The face cloth lay neatly folded, just as Jesus had laid it aside. YOU BET! THEY BELIEVED!

Now, they too, headed back to town, discussing as they walked, what they had seen. Excitement added wings to their feet, and soon they were telling all over, what had taken place. Fear of the Jews made them careful who they spoke to, but even so, there were a goodly number of people to visit with.

Everyone was still governed by the fear generated by the crucifixion, so they quietly gathered where there was room for all. They wished both to discuss what they had seen and heard, and see if Jesus would really meet them. Many were quite skeptical, and Thomas didn't even show up.

Suddenly, Jesus was standing in their midst without even bothering to use the door. The same power that had allowed Him to come right through the grave clothes, allowed Him to come right through the walls.

In spite of the fact that they loved Him, fear tied their stomachs in knots. Jesus spoke comfortingly, "Look, My friends, I surely wouldn't hurt you! I've come in peace. If there are any doubts in your minds that it is I, look here."

He turned His hands up and extended them. The prints of the nails were clearly visible. Since the anointing in Heaven was finished, they no longer bled. The scars were all that remained. He also pulled His clothing apart to bare His side where the spear wound could be seen.

"Now, My friends, as God the Father has sent Me, so now,

I'm sending you. You will need to be guided by the Holy Spirit so—" He blew upon them and said, "Receive the Holy Ghost!"[19]"

They would still need the Baptism of the Holy Spirit at Pentecost, but from now on, all Christians would have this particular portion of the Holy Spirit from salvation on. This would open their understanding of the scriptures.

When the rest of the disciples found Thomas, he flatly refused to believe them. "Aw, you're having a pipe dream," he told them. "This has shaken you up so much that you're losing your sanity! I'd have to stick my finger into the nail wounds, and my hand into His side before I'd believe!"

Eight days later, he got his chance. Jesus appeared among them, and singled Thomas right out.

"Come here, Thomas, and probe My wounds," He ordered. "See, here are My hands and My side—and you can even play with My feet if you want to!"

Thomas was crushed, and could only answer, "Jesus, You are my Lord and my God."

"Yes, Thomas, now you can believe, since you have seen Me. What would you have done if you had been born a thousand years from now? My heart goes out to those who will believe in Me without ever having seen Me!"

A few days earlier, Jesus appeared to Peter, who needed a little one on one counseling. The things Peter had said and done the night of the crucifixion were weighing heavily on his conscience, and Jesus needed to help him out.

"Look, Peter, I told you that you would deny Me. You didn't have the Holy Spirit to give you strength. No one can handle the forces of Satan in his own power.

"You don't have to earn points with Me. I earned your salvation so you could have it free. I do expect you to do your best. Where you fall short, then My unmerited favor takes over. Forget the past, My friend, It's forgiven. Move on to the future! I've got a lot of work for you."

Two other friends were walking along the road to Emmaus when they met Jesus on the road. He withheld their ability to recognize Him as He began to question them about their fervent conversation.

Cleopas looked at Him in surprise and asked, "Man, what did You do, just hit town? I thought everyone had heard about the crucifixion of Jesus of Nazareth. We even thought He might be the Messiah! Some of our friends have been telling us that He has risen from the dead, but that is kind of hard to believe."

Jesus replied, "Why?"

Cleopas looked up in surprise and answered with a dull, "Huh?"

Jesus repeated, "Why? He said He would, didn't He?"

The two men looked a little puzzled and replied, "I guess we don't know."

"Well, even if He hadn't, which He did," returned Jesus, "the scriptures say He will rise. David says that the Father wouldn't allow His body to see corruption or leave Him in Hades, nor, for that matter, allow a bone of His body to be broken.

"Isaiah describes what His body looked like, before crucifixion was even a method of execution. The scriptures say that He would be lifted up.

"Some of the later prophets say that the Jewish people, in the last days, will look upon Him whom they have pierced.

"Besides, what do you think sacrifices point to? They point forward to the perfect sacrifice of the Messiah. And since the Messiah is the bodily portion of the Godhead, God surely couldn't leave Him in the grave, could He? This was the only way Jesus could receive the glory due Him!"

Jesus acted as though He would go on, but by now, He really had their attention. And since it was getting dark, they asked, "Why don't you spend the night with us, since it is late?"

Still, it wasn't until they were about to eat supper that they recognized Him; and that when He blessed, broke the bread, and passed it around. As soon as they recognized Him, He was gone.

The two men risked the dangers of the road at night, because they couldn't wait until morning to tell what had happened to them. Upon entering Jerusalem, they arrived just in time to hear about Peter's experience with the Lord. Everyone was having a glorious time sharing experiences when the Lord appeared with them.

In spite of everything, there were still some of them who were terrified, and thought He was a spirit, or ghost.

Jesus said, "Oh come on! Don't get shook up! A spirit doesn't have flesh and bones. Come feel Me. I've got a real material body. It's just a little higher quality than yours! Yes, I am your God, and scripture says God is a Spirit. Don't make it complicated. I have spiritual flesh." To demonstrate even further, He ate a piece of fish and honey.

After eating, Jesus began to explain to them just why He had to die. "Folks, I was sinless when I died. In other words, I didn't have to die. However, My unearned death pays for your earned one, so you don't have to die eternally. You will die physically, but you'll be raised at the end of the age. All you have to do to be saved is repent, and ask Me for forgiveness. I'll do, or have done, the rest. That is why I had to die and rise again."

Even with the Lord truly risen, it still seemed like the apostles were rather at loose ends, and the ones who were fishermen decided to go back to their old trade.

As is often the case in a situation like this, it didn't work. They fished all night, and caught nothing. The next morning, Jesus appeared standing on the shore. "Have you caught anything?" He shouted.

"Not a thing!" they answered.

"Go back out and cast your net on the right-hand side," Jesus ordered.

Of course, 'ol' Luie the Lip' Peter had to inform Him, "But we've fished all night, and all we've caught is a cold and blisters; however, if You insist, we'll put in a few more hours."

The boat began to turn and Peter muttered, "He don't even know that you always cast the net on the left side!"

This time, the nets, lowered on the wrong side, came up

so full that they had to drag them to shore, and still, they didn't break.

John whispered in awe to Peter, "That has to be the Lord."

Again, typical of Peter, he just dove into the water and swam to shore instead of waiting for the boats.

Jesus had a nice fire going and fish done to a turn, along with bread. "Come and dine, My friends," He invited.

After they had eaten, Jesus waved His hand toward the large pile of fish, and asked, "Simon, do you love Me more than these?"

Peter replied, "Sure Lord, You know how I feel about You."

"Feed My lambs," Jesus returned and added, "Simon, do you love Me more than these?"

Peter winced, but came on a little stronger this time, "Sure Lord, You know I love You."

"OK, Simon, then feed My sheep." Then for the third time, He asked, "Simon, do you love Me more than these fish?"

Peter was getting antsy now, and replied, "Lord, You know all things. You know that I love You."

"Then Simon, you have to feed My sheep. This is how you do it. You must preach the gospel to all the world, baptizing them in the name of the Father, the Son, and the Holy Ghost. One of the signs that will follow those who do this will be power! They will cast out demons, speak in new tongues, be impervious to poison, and lay hands on the sick who will then recover.

Forty days after His resurrection, He stood on the Mount of Olives, spoke to His followers, and told them, "You must wait in Jerusalem for the Baptism of the Holy Spirit. You are weak now, but this will give you the power you will need."

As He was speaking, He began to slowly rise from the Earth. With a wave of His hand to them, He lifted high enough to enter into a cloud, and out of sight.

Michael and Gabriel appeared and asked, "Hey you guys, why are you standing around craning your necks? Jesus will come back just the same way He left. In the mean time, you've got a great deal to do."

It was, indeed, a much happier and different group of people who headed back to Jerusalem from Olivet, than the ones who had wept their way down from Golgotha!

ENDNOTES

[1] Ezekiel 1:22 26 pictures the throne of God, as does Revelation 15:2, which adds fire to the great diamond upon which it sits. Ezekiel calls it a terrible crystal. The word he uses is qerach, which means a substance resembling rock, crystal, frost, or ice. Who hasn't heard diamonds called ice, and seen what appeared to be fire flash within then when they caught the light.

[2] Ezekiel 28:11-19 could not be directed to a human being. God has to be speaking to Lucifer, the covering cherub. Verse 13 speaks of taberets and pipes. He was in charge of music. Cherubim upon the arc of the Covenant portrayed the true covering cherubim in Heaven—God's honor guard.

[3] Creatures described in Ezekiel 1:5-11. Yes, every portion of them is symbolic of something, but this gives us no right to deny their reality. Creatures as grotesque as these live right here on Earth today.

[4] We reject the notion that Beelzebub is another name for Lucifer. Beelzebub is merely the prince of the demons. Lucifer reigns over his entire evil kingdom.

[5] We also reject the belief that Apollyon is another of Lucifer's names. Apollyon is the angel of the bottomless pit. He is imprisoned in the Abyss—Tartarus. By rank, he rules the angels in solitary confinement. He is to mindlessly vicious to be allowed on Earth.

[6] Ezekiel 28:13—Heaven is split up just as the Mosaic tabernacle was. This is the Heavenly Eden. Probably, the earthly Eden was also split this way. The Garden was placed eastward in Eden. We have the throne room—Mountain of God, as the Holy of Holies. The Garden of God is the Holy Place, and the District of Eden is the Outer Court. Note the chapter entitled "Soul Sleep" in this author's book: "To Heaven By Way of Your Boot Straps".

[7] Read Chapter nine, Sovereignty of God in this authors book: To Heaven by Way of Your Boot Straps.

[8] Seven is the number of completion. Eight is the number of new beginning and freedom. Sunday is depicted in Prophecy as the eighth day. We refer you to Chapter 4 of To Heaven By Way of Your Boot Straps. The first seven in any series in scripture portray the dispensation before the age of grace.

[9] Psalms 8:9 Man was created a little lower than the angels. He was to reach a point where all that God had created would be under him. That would have put him second only to the Trinity.

[10] All creatures were created to eat vegetable foods (plant eaters) Genesis 1:29-30. After the flood of Noah's time, men were given permission to eat meat (Genesis 9:3). Subsequent laws limited this to the clean animals. Christ's death on the cross fulfilled the Mosaic Law, and all flesh was then cleansed.

[11] Luke 21:10

[12] Israel

[13] Becomes a nation

[14] The Lord is about to come

[15] Luke 7:37-38 and Matthew 26:7-13

[16] Luke 22:35-36

[17] Psalms 22:17

[18] In the story of the rich man and Lazarus (Luke 16:19-31), we see the righteous and wicked dead both in confinement. Due to the fact that they are (or were) three part beings, in death, they are two part beings. As such, they are recognizable as well as capable of sensation and feeling.

[19] John 20:22 and Luke 24:45

ISBN 1412027501-0